THE KIDNAPPING OF CODY MOSS

Smoky Mountain Suspense Book One

Sara L. Foust

The Kidnapping of Cody Moss, Smoky Mountain Suspense Book One
©2019 Sara L. Foust

Published by Silver Lining Literary Services
106 Offutt Rd.
Clinton, TN 37716
www.saralfoust.com

Printed in the United States of America

The persons and events portrayed in this work of fiction are the creations of the author, and any resemblance to persons living or dead is purely coincidental.

ISBN 978-1-7329047-1-2

Scripture quoted is from the King James Version of the Bible, which is in public domain.
©2019 Cover Design by Sara L. Foust

For Abby

My energetic, artistic, beautiful firstborn. I love your imagination, your love of late nights, your creativity, and your kind heart. I am so proud that you are proud to be who you are—exactly as God made you. I love you. Stay sticky, alabooboo.

And we know that all things work together for good to them that love God, to them who are called according to *his* purpose.

Romans 8:38 KJV

Chapter One

Why couldn't she just say yes?

Annalise unlaced her hiking boots and wiped sweat from her brow with her shirtsleeve. This job offer was everything she ever wanted. Why couldn't the little voice in the back of her mind just finally say yes? She groaned as she dug for her keys in the bottom of her pack.

Hiking in the fall was her favorite, when the crunch of leaves underfoot released a rich, earthy smell and the sun played in rainbowed treetops. This year's color peak was still two weeks away, and the cooler temperatures had yet to arrive. At Annalise's feet, Millie sat, her ridiculously long tongue lolling out of her half-smiling doggy mouth.

"Come on, Millicent. In ya go."

Millie didn't hesitate to leap into the open truck.

"Good girl."

With her best beagle friend in the passenger seat, head hanging out the window into the fall air, and a good couple hours' hiking under her belt, Annalise's mind should've felt lighter. But no matter what she did, the weight wouldn't leave. She had to make a decision about the new job by Friday, and she hadn't even told Dave yet. Why had she waited so long to have this discussion with her husband?

Annalise slipped the small pack holding her badge and gun into the center console, took a swig of ice-cold water, and aimed her truck for home. If she hurried, she could have dinner on the table before Dave got there and maybe, for the first time in weeks, they would be able to share a meal and a conversation. Her stomach clenched at the thought of asking him to move, again. He seemed so content living in Norris. And he'd worked so hard to landscape their backyard and bring her vision to life. They'd had thirteen months in their new oasis, and now she would be asking him to leave it. For her career. Again.

And what about the new clientele he had managed to build? If they moved now, he'd be starting his heating and air conditioning business all over again. Again.

Norris was great. Everything she'd hoped it would be. Safe. Quaint. Filled with friendly East Tennesseans and genuine smiles. And a job that offered full benefits, a great retirement program, a salary that provided all they needed, and coworkers she had come to love in the past two years.

But.

But what?

What was it about this life she'd dreamed of that left her wanting? Wasn't this exactly where she'd planned on being by her thirtieth birthday in a few weeks?

Her phone beeped with an incoming message. At the next stop sign, she glanced at it.

"Going to be late again. Sorry. Love ya."

Oh, great. "Love ya, too, babe." She dropped the phone into the cup holder, gave Millie a passing pat, and turned left. Two more turns and she'd be home. By herself. For the rest of the evening, if she guessed correctly.

When had Dave taken to saying love ya instead of I love you? Somewhere along the line, it slipped in, and Annalise couldn't even begin to pinpoint the date, time, or reason. Should she worry?

She laughed, and Millie cocked her head sideways and looked at her. "What? I know it was a ridiculous thought too. You don't have to point it out to me."

And it was silly. Wasn't it? Dave was, always had been, a wonderful husband. Patient, kind, hardworking. A deacon in their church before they left Memphis. A role model for the young men. She shook her head. That train of thought needed to run out of track. And then she needed to put the poor train out of its misery, wherever trains went to retire.

A hot shower massaged some of the thoughts from her mind, and the sliver of New York style cheesecake she'd hidden in the back of the fridge helped finish them off. She took a cup of decaf with hazelnut creamer to their backyard and settled into the swing hammock to watch the evening fall.

Millie followed her each step like usual, sinking to her stomach to watch the birds flit to and from the feeder. Her eyebrows tracked the birds' movements, first left, then right, up then down. What would Millie watch when most of them flew south in a couple weeks?

Annalise was supposed to be at that stage where she stayed put. Threw down some roots, had some babies, and watched those delicate roots turn to massive oak trees. Why was her heart pulling her toward the Smokies? Toward this new idea and an old friend?

Her phone jingled. She picked it up without looking at the caller ID. "I was just thinking about you."

Her captain's voice sounded through the line. "You were, eh? I hope it was good things."

Oh my gosh, not Zach. "Sir, I am so sorry. Thought you were someone else." Her cheeks burned as hot as a hundred-degree-day-at-the-lake sunburn.

"I need you at 1500 Dairy Pond Road. Had a bit of an incident come in from 9-1-1. My on-duty officer is working a car accident out toward the dam, and I need to join him. Do you mind coming in on your evening off?"

"Yes, sir. Or no, sir." She chuckled. "I can be there in ten."

A bit of an incident? No details. A cat in a tree? A fender bender? A missing newspaper? Wonder what her best friend Zach was up to this evening? Maybe something as benign as her case would probably turn out to be, but at least he'd had some exciting cases in Gatlinburg recently. Nothing bad seemed to ever happen in this tucked-away utopia.

And that was a good thing. Wasn't it?

Chapter Two

Zach Leebow flagged at least the hundredth car around the fringe of the newest mudslide and shook the rain from his sleeve. It was coming down faster than they would be able to counteract soon. All they needed on the upcoming weekend was to have Highway 321 closed down. Their wettest East Tennessee spring on record had continued right on through a scorching, thunderstorm-filled summer and into the beginning of fall. And all their good ole East Tennessee red clay mud had started sliding months ago and never stopped. It was just a matter of which section would go next.

What would Annalise be doing right about now? Probably headed home to cook her husband a hearty supper. Too bad Jo was visiting friends back home all week. He missed her home cooking. A twinge of guilt poked his empty stomach. Did he miss her too?

He rolled his shoulders to shake off the rain and the gloomy thought. He'd just have to eat fast food again. Ick. He was sick of too-thin burgers and cholesterol sticks.

His days of traffic cop duty were coming to a rapid close. He couldn't wait. He had met the other member of the new team, Kirk Johnson, a couple weeks ago. The man's reputation had preceded him. If he could get Annalise on board, they'd have the perfect team for this new endeavor.

A rumble echoed through the channels between the mountains where the road slithered through their peaks. The road crew. Good. Maybe they could get things stabilized so he could go home.

He didn't mean to sound so burnt-out and grouchy. But the truth was, he was. He'd never intended to stay low-level in the Gatlinburg police force. Routine traffic stops, crowd control, and domestic disputes grew boring almost as soon as he started handling them straight out of the academy. That was seven years ago.

Thankful for his job? Of course. But he'd always had a feeling there was something more he was meant to do. This new task force was God's gift to him. Though it wasn't something he'd envisioned, simply because it was a brand-new idea, all the details fit him perfectly. They would be in charge of investigating crimes and disappearances in the backcountry of the Great Smoky Mountains. The place he loved most in the whole world.

A car zipped by, faster than slow, and soaked the few remaining dry spots Zach had. Lovely.

The ground began to tremble as the tractors approached, and with his next breath, they rounded the corner. A slow procession that brought a smile to his face. The knobby-tired, big-bucketed cavalry had arrived. His stomach rumbled its agreement with the thought of getting to go home in the next hour. Hopefully.

He held up both hands and brought traffic to a full, grinding halt. One frustrated motorist honked. He was sure others wanted to and probably cursed him from the soundproof safety of their vehicles. The men on the tractors waved and began scraping up the goopy, soupy mess of clay mud, rock, fallen orange leaves, and bits of murdered plants and saplings.

The radio under his slicker crackled to life. "Officer requesting backup on the 500 block of the Little Pigeon. Nonemergency traffic. First officer available."

Zach gave it a few minutes. No one replied. Fifteen more minutes and the crew would have this small slide under control. His shift had ended forty-five minutes ago, but on a night like this, with the county and the sky going crazy, he couldn't turn a blind eye and head off to his warm, dry bed. He pulled his arm in through the gaping sleeve of his poncho and depressed the button. "I'll be clear on the highway in ten to fifteen. If no one else becomes available, I'll head up that way."

"Ten-four, Officer Leebow. Thanks. Keep us posted."

So much for dinner.

What was going on up there? Nonemergency was good, but if it wasn't an emergency, why on earth did they need backup?

Half an hour later, Zach stepped out of his cruiser, slipped the slicker on once more, and strode to Officer Colby's side. "What's up?"

The young man, fresh from the academy, turned a pale face and dilated pupils toward him. With a single finger attached to a shaking hand, Colby pointed down the embankment.

In the fading light, Zach couldn't positively identify the black mass at the bottom. But he had his suspicions this wasn't a dead bear. He scooched down the mud-slick bank, and the smell of rotting flesh invaded his nostrils. Thoughts of eating vanished instantly.

He turned his flashlight beam toward the lump.

A torn, black t-shirt and blue jeans confirmed the humanity of the body.

Zach's stomach clenched. It wasn't his first death scene, but he never got used to them. "Colby, call dispatch and tell them to get the M.E. and an ambulance out here. Now."

He searched the area surrounding the face-down body and found nothing, then he turned his light toward the creek. Normally calm and shallow, tonight it raged, licking the man's boots. The last bout of heavy rain three hours ago must've pushed the body up on shore then receded as the water traveled downstream off the mountain.

Zach glanced up, but it was too dark to tell just how close the clouds were to unleashing another torrential downpour. If the drizzle continued, there should be nothing to worry about. But, if the sky decided to open up again, would they lose the body to the water?

"Gonna be at least an hour," Colby called down the hill. "County's red right now and the M.E. is in Knoxville."

Great. Zach watched the edge of the water lapping at the dead man's hiking boots. If it rose even an inch, he'd have to move the body and hope he didn't disturb any evidence. He slipped on some latex gloves and prayed.

Zach snapped some photos with his phone then knelt and felt the man's pockets. No wallet. No rectangular shapes like a cell phone. Possibly a flashlight in the front pocket, under the body, and there was definitely something in the other pocket, but without removing it, he couldn't be sure what it was.

Purposefully avoiding looking too hard at the gaping wound on the back of the head, he passed his light over the shoulders, forearms, and hands. Scratches. Some abrasions at the base of the neck on either side. But nothing that screamed, to him at least, of a major altercation before the fatal gunshot wound to the head.

The water now danced at the man's ankles.

Zach grunted, a moment of indecision giving him pause. But it would be better to preserve possession of the body and risk contamination than to let the body sink beneath the waves again. Right? If he'd been washed down the creek a ways, chances were most of the evidence would be gone anyway.

He looped his hands under the body's arms. *Lord, please keep him, and any evidence that may still be here, intact.*

Zach hefted and pulled until the body was a safer distance from the water, then he rushed back to check the ground where the man had lain. What was this? He pulled his phone back out, took a few photos, and then gingerly picked up the sliver of paper.

A corner of a trail map, laminated by what Zach figured was packing tape on the intact edges, lay in the palm of his hand. Bingo. An actual clue.

A flash of lightning lit the sky, followed immediately by a tremendous boom of thunder. Seconds later the sky broke.

Chapter Three

Annalise stopped her cruiser in front of a beautiful English-cottage-style home framed by sugar maples sporting brilliant crimson leaves illuminated by numerous yard lights. How many times had she admired this very one when driving by?

She was met at the front steps by a shorter, dark-haired woman clutching the chubby hand of a blond-haired toddler with round cheeks. "Thank goodness you're here, ma'am. You have to get that infernal thing out of here."

Great. Snake or skunk this time? "Can you tell me where it is?"

The woman pointed a quivering finger at a child's red wagon sitting forgotten and forlorn across the wide yard. "There. Coulda killed my boy here."

Snake then. Probably nonvenomous. Usually were. What were the chances it was even still in the wagon? In any other town, animal control or wildlife control would handle a situation like this. Not the police department. But in a city of less than fifteen hundred people with a crime rate 53% below the national average, chasing snakes, stray dogs, and trying to free the good citizens of skunks in mating season without getting sprayed were often the most exciting parts of their days.

Annalise picked up a long, forked stick and peeked over the side, shining her flashlight into the small space. What in the world? That was no snake. Or skunk. Or anything else alive. She tossed a glance toward the mother and her son waiting on the covered front porch. No wonder the mom had been so worried.

Holding up one finger, she trotted to her car and grabbed a pair of disposable gloves and a bag. Just in case. And returned to the wagon. She snapped a few photos then lifted the handgun gently and slipped it into a brown paper bag.

So strange. How on earth did it get into the little boy's wagon? And where had it come from? Her thoughts carried her to her car and back to the porch. "Ma'am, who found the weapon?"

"My son. I already said that."

"Yes, of course. And when was this?"

"Right before I called 9-1-1."

She would have to check the call logs and note the exact time of that call. "Any clue where the gun came from?"

The mother shook her head.

"Have you noticed anyone walking by today or maybe late last night?"

"Nobody other than the school kids this morning and this afternoon."

Surely none of those innocent, white-collar-parented children would drop a loaded weapon into a kid's wagon and hope nothing bad happened. Annalise shook her head. She knew these kids from her hours spent in the halls of the middle school. None of them would be so careless. Even as she thought it, she knew she was being foolish. "When was the last time your son played with the wagon?"

"Yesterday evening. Just before sunset."

"Thank you, ma'am. We'll be in touch if we have any other questions."

"Come on, Joey." The mother pulled her reluctant son into the house and shut the door, not bothering to thank Annalise for her service.

There was a simple explanation for this. Had to be. Someone had lost their handgun while walking by.

And it happened to bounce into the wagon sitting fifteen feet off the road.

Okay, someone had tossed it out the window. Like accidentally losing a shoe.

Right.

If someone had tossed the gun, it meant they were getting rid of it. And it would make so much more sense to toss it into the dumpster or a body of water. And there were only a few reasons to get rid of a gun that way. Around here, people sold them for the money they knew they were worth. Not tossed them. Unless they were in possession of them illegally, which was a crime. Or the weapon was used in a crime. Or both.

Annalise aimed her vehicle for the station, but driving away didn't leave the sense of curious anxiety behind. This was a safe town. Not a dump-your-unwanted-killing-items-on-the-side-of-the-road town. Not a put-an-innocent-child-in-harm's-way town.

"Hey, captain," Annalise said as she stepped through the doorway into the cool, concrete-floored bay area at the fire/police station. "Back already?"

"Yeah, wasn't near as bad as we thought. One headed to the hospital with chest pains, and the vehicle needs a funeral, but everyone should be okay."

"That's good." She sat in the chair opposite him. "This call was interesting."

"Not a critter call?"

"No, sir."

She opened the bag and held it under his nose.

"Whoa. Where'd that come from?"

"I asked the same thing, sir."

He laced his fingers under his chin, raising both index fingers to cover his lips. "Hmmm."

She knew better than to interrupt his musings.

"Have you decided on that new job yet?"

Annalise's heart skipped a beat. "What?"

"The new job."

"How did you—"

His smile was genuine. "I know a lot of things, Annalise. It's a good opportunity for you."

It was. "I would miss all of you terribly."

"We will miss you too."

Will? As in he's already saying goodbye? "I don't know…"

"Yes, you do. Opportunities like this one don't come around every day." He leaned back in his chair, as if the conversation, and the decision, were completed. "As for that," he pointed to the bag, "send it to the lab. Fingerprints, gunshot residue, ballistics. The works."

"Yes, sir."

"I've got a feeling we may have an actual crime on our hands, young Annalise."

She did too.

Thunder carried in a massive line of clouds before Annalise made it home to her dark house. Empty yet again. She darted through the sheet of raindrops the size of grapes. The full color of fall wouldn't be so full if it kept up like this. On the front porch, she sank into the swing and wrung rainwater from her heavy hair.

Where was her husband tonight? Shouldn't the storm—or at least the dark—preclude working on someone's outdoor heating unit? It had in the past. Had the rules changed somewhere and she just wasn't aware of it?

Are you talking about heating and air work or life, Annalise? Zach's gentle voice sounded in her mind. Both, Zach. Both.

Speak of the devil.

Whoa, when had she begun to think of Dave as the devil? She shook her head as his headlights cut off. She didn't. Just a passing thought spawned by an age-old saying.

He raced up the walkway, receiving the same dousing she'd gotten minutes before. No, she didn't think of him as the devil. He was handsome, kind, and patient. When they'd married eight years ago, she couldn't ever imagine a day when she'd have half the thoughts she had now. It was her investigative, creative mind playing tricks on her. Conning her into negative thoughts when she knew the truth. Dave was a good man. An honest man.

She forced her voice to sound like freshly uncorked champagne bubbles, when the emotions carrying it felt more like day-old soda. Flat, tasteless, worn out. "Hey, babe."

Dave jumped and spun toward her.

"Sorry. Didn't mean to startle you." When had things become so stiff between them? So awkward.

He forced his it's okay, I'm tired smile. "What are you doing out here?"

"Drying off. Thinking."

"Oh."

Wasn't he going to ask what she was thinking about? He would have in the old days. In the early days. In the good days. Were they no longer good days? "Come sit with me."

He didn't meet her gaze. "I'm all wet. Let me go change first."

"I'm wet too." She held the front of her uniform out from her chest as a demonstration. "Look, I need to talk to you about something."

He sucked a squeaky breath through his front teeth.

Annalise rolled her eyes. She hated that sound. When had the cute little nuances about her husband become things to hate? To drive her insane and make her want to shove plugs into her ear canals?

"I'm awful tired. Can we talk another time?"

The blood drained from her head. In less time than it took the raindrops to plop from the eaves to the ground, the steadiness of her life whooshed away from her. What did it mean that he was unwilling to sit with her? To listen to her? That he was too tired to spend a moment with her? Before she could reply, he disappeared inside. The clicking of the front door closing sounded so hollow. So loud. So final.

Chapter Four

Zach pulled his uniform from the dryer and sniffed deeply. Three washes and a cup of bleach and it still smelled like death and dirty sweat-socks. He'd have to put in a request for a new one or make the ones he had last until the new job started. Washing laundry every other day would be a pain, but it was better than smelling like a corpse. What was he talking about? He only had two days left.

Speaking of corpse, maybe he should call the ME and find out about their John Doe from the creek. Surely something in the man's pockets could help them identify him. Or at least point them in the direction toward the murder scene.

Upstream, obviously. But where?

He slid into a uniform he retrieved from the bedroom floor. It smelled much better than the one from the night prior but not exactly sunshine fresh. It would have to do. He pulled up the photos from the creek and swiped until he found the one of the shard of map. If he could figure out which one this had come from, they'd have a clue.

But the trail maps for the Smokies outnumbered the bears. How on earth could he find the right one? He needed help.

Annalise picked up on the third ring.

"Hey, whatcha doing?"

"Getting ready to drive some evidence to Nashville. Why? What's up?"

"I was hoping you could help me with something."

"Can we do it on the road?"

"Nah, but it can wait. Still want some company? I could tag along and bring everything from the Gatlinburg department too. Make a day of it."

"Sure. I hate driving alone. Well, you know that." She giggled.

Yes, he did. He knew just about everything there was to know about Annalise Baker. "Come pick me up. Have you accepted the job yet?"

There was a long pause, in which he could picture her gnawing on her cheek like she always had. "Not yet. I still haven't told Dave."

"Seriously? They want an answer by Friday. You can't pass this up, Lise. You just can't."

"I don't know…"

Was something more going on here than she had told him? He'd get her to open up on the three-hour drive. "See you soon."

"Be there in twenty."

Spending the day in the car with Zach certainly beat spending it alone. But, at the same time, one look at her and Zach would know something wasn't right. How could she avoid telling him the truth? She didn't even know what the truth was yet.

Zach met her at the curb, a grocery bag hanging from one arm and a doughnut and coffees in a cardboard drink holder in the other. He swung open the door, somehow.

"How on earth did you manage…Never mind." This was Zach she was talking to, after all. The food-is-always-a-priority man. The one who dreamed in shades of meat doneness and tones of chocolate cakes.

She knew. Because he'd told her all of his dreams, every morning during college and when they were separated in different police academies. After she'd married Dave, those phone calls had slowed and then stopped. She never realized she missed them until now.

"Coffee. Fat-free half and half and two Splenda packets."

She took the cup he offered. "Thanks."

Zach slid into the seat, managing not to spill a drop of his coffee nor lose balance in any way. He'd always been the nimble one.

Her, not so much. How she'd made it this far in life without a broken bone or two was beyond her.

He flashed her a chocolatey-glazed grin. "So, what's up with you and Dave?"

Well, just diving right in, eh, old friend? "Nothing. What makes you think something's up?" She could slap her forehead. Her high pitch with a break in the middle of the sentence gave her away.

"You have a tell."

"Ugh, I know." Her shoulders stooped. "Listen, I don't wanna talk about it. Okay?"

Zach nodded. And smacked another bite of doughnut.

"Do you think you could chew a little less like a cow and a little more like a human being who has at least the bare minimum of manners?"

"Hmm, oh, sure thing."

He leaned in close and chewed slowly.

She laughed and shoved his shoulder. "Seriously? Are you still twelve?"

"Mmm-hmm."

Hopefully traffic would cooperate with them, and she wouldn't have to listen to his chomping on the way home with dinner too. She zipped onto 40W and hit cruise control. Zach's chewing ended, but his words didn't resume. What was up with him? She could never get him quiet this long. "We going to drive the whole way in silence?"

"You said you didn't want to talk about it."

"Oh, good grief. Let it go, okay?" Her tone had more bite to it than she intended. But she couldn't voice her fears. Then they would be real.

"Got a body."

"What?"

"A body. A murder."

Zach always did know how to make a conversation U-turn and get a chuckle from her. "Oh, yeah? Where did you find him or her?"

"Little Pigeon, after the rainstorm. Well, more like during the rainstorm, last night."

"Got any leads?"

"He was shot. That's about all we know. What's in the bag?"

The bag? Oh, right. Another U-turn. "A gun."

"What's so special about it?"

"It was found in a child's little red wagon. You know, the metal ones?"

"Weird. But really worth driving to Nashville yourself?"

"Let's just say I have a hunch."

"That's why the Smoky Mountain Investigative Force needs you."

"I don't know, Zach."

"Sure you do. You know you want the job. Something is worrying you. Which brings us back to Dave."

She shot him a look that she hoped said, stop it, right now, I'm serious.

He held his hands up in surrender. "But we aren't talking about that. SMIF."

"What?"

"Not a great acronym, if you ask me."

Oh, Smoky Mountain Investigative Force. Sheesh. This road was making her a bit dizzy. "No, you're right about that one."

"But it will be a great job. I have a hunch too. This body started out somewhere up in the mountains and washed down with the storm."

"Uh-huh. Sounds like a possibility. It rained a monsoon last night."

"Map. Well, a piece of one."

"Zach, it's a good thing I love you."

He swung his gaze on her and pinned her with his stare.

Ha! She'd gotten him to pause in his zig-zag of random thoughts. "You're making my head spin."

"Sorry. I'm good like that. It's the handsomeness that gets most."

Laughing felt good after so many straight hours of worrying about Dave and the new job and the other woman—

Whoa, there was another woman now? Thanks, imagination.

Silence entombed the car. Annalise switched the radio onto K-Love and tapped her finger to the beat of a Zach Williams song. Good. Something upbeat and distracting and not depressing like her muddled mind.

Zach pointed at the radio. "Zach."

"Um, yep."

"Love him."

She glanced at his profile. "Me too." And she did. She really, really loved him. Always had.

Always would. Through the irritating chomping and the crazy conversations. And especially the way he knew her like no one else and never judged. "Had any interesting dreams lately?"

Chapter Five

Why did Annalise telling him she loved him, in that casual, non-strange, non-romantic way, make his insides feel so odd? In all their years of friendship, she hadn't ever said that. He'd known it. Love, like a brother. Or an annoying uncle she tolerated because she had to.

But she didn't have to. She chose to.

And he was thankful for that. What would he do if she stopped choosing to?

"Zach? You still there?"

"Hmm?"

"Are you ready for lunch?"

Good, safe subject. "Always ready for food."

"Right. Dumb question."

Annalise could run from his earlier, not-dumb question all she wanted, but he knew something was up. Call it instinct. A hunch. Whatever. There was a problem in her life. And it involved Dave.

If Dave had hurt Annalise somehow, he'd never forgive the man.

Annalise pulled off the interstate and aimed for a Hardee's near Cookeville. Halfway or so. He'd have to push a little harder to get past her iron-firm shell. Strange. Normally she was an open book with him. Well, she used to be anyway. He had to admit their visits and phone calls had grown sparser with each passing year Annalise had been married. But this must be really bad if she couldn't even begin to talk to him about it. She knew he was a safe place for her to land her worries and fears. A low growl escaped his lips.

"You okay there?" Annalise chuckled.

"Yep. Just hungry." Which was true. He was always hungry. But angry and worried too. He was an investigator. Not supposed to jump to conclusions. It was awfully hard not to when his best friend's heart may be on the line.

He just needed a new tactic. "I'm breaking up with Jo."

Annalise veered into the parking space crooked. "What? Why? I thought you two were pretty serious."

"It just doesn't feel right."

"Seriously, Zach? She is an amazing woman."

"She is."

"So what is it?"

"I don't know. She's not the one. I mean, how did you know with Dave?" Ah, there, sneaky.

Was she going to answer him? He tapped the windowsill with his index finger. One. Two… Fifteen. He glanced at her profile.

A tear slipped down her cheek.

Atta girl. Come on, Annalise. Talk to me.

"He was kind and generous and hardworking and sweet. I just knew." She swallowed hard. "All right, Zach. You win. I'm worried."

"I know. How come?"

"He's been working all sorts of crazy hours and making excuses for coming home late. And last night I tried to talk to him about the job but…"

"But what?"

"It…He brushed me off. He's never acted like he didn't want to spend time with me. Until last night." She sighed. "I have no proof, no reason to doubt his loyalty, but I can feel it. Something's wrong."

"Could be a million things. Maybe he knows he is about to lose his job and he doesn't want to disappoint you."

"Maybe."

"Maybe he has cancer and doesn't want to scare you."

"Zach!"

"Hey, I'm just saying it's a possibility."

"Right."

Even with her staring straight ahead, he saw her eyes roll. "Maybe he has a surprise planned for you and is trying not to spill the beans."

"I kinda doubt it." She gnawed on her cheek.

"What is it?"

"There's been…distance between us, in the bedroom. You know?"

"Ouch. Okay, yeah, let's not go there." Anywhere but there. What advice could he give in that department? Zero. Nada. Zilch. That's what. Call him old fashioned, but he was waiting for God to send him a wife first. But, he couldn't imagine being in Dave's shoes and giving Annalise the cold shoulder in any room of their house. Especially not the bedr— He shook his head. Not an image he needed to allow to materialize.

"What if…"

Her cheek would need stitches if she didn't spit the thought out soon.

"…there's another woman?"

Heat flared up his throat, kissing his thoughts with smoldering anger. "There'd better not be."

Zach's big-brother protectiveness over her had always made her feel safe. Like knowing he had her back meant there was at least one safe place in the world for her to hide.

He couldn't protect her from this though. Hard to keep her from her own emotions and imagination attacking.

"Be nice. He is still my husband." What was she saying? Of course he was. "I have no proof of anything! What am I talking about?" She hit the steering wheel with her palm. "Forget I said anything."

"Yeah, 'cause that worked so well before." He winked.

She smiled. "You're a pest. But, seriously, you can't be mad at Dave for my crazy thoughts."

"Righto."

"Your tone gives you away, friend. Dave is a good man. Honest. Dependable. He would never do what I am accusing him of."

Zach's tone softened. "I can be mad at him for making you even think it in the first place, can't I?"

She hadn't looked at it that way before. "I suppose."

"So what are you going to do about it?"

"Me?"

"Your marriage is in trouble, Annalise. If you don't address it now, and things get worse, you will regret not talking to him now."

Sometimes Zach knowing her so well was irritating. "When did you get so wise?"

"Dunno. Just comes natural, I guess."

Her laughter floated out the window and probably rolled around on the leaf-dotted asphalt. "Thanks for making me smile, Zach."

"My pleasure." He opened his door. "Now, what about that food?"

Annalise swallowed another refreshing sip of her soda. What was it about fountain drinks that was so much better than bottled or canned?

"Why are we going to Nashville?" Zach took another massive bite of his burger.

"Um, the gun."

"Yeah, but why not have it tested at our lab?"

"Oh. Ours is booked solid, plus we aren't sure it was used in a crime, so there's no way to expedite it. But Nashville said they could get results to me in seventy-two hours."

"Why is it so important in the first place?"

"You haven't worked in Norris."

"What's that got to do with it?"

"I live and work in a modern-day Mayberry. Nothing more than an occasional parking ticket or a missing pet happens here. It's…wonderful."

"I don't believe you."

She didn't believe her either. She sighed. "It's boring."

He clapped his hands. "Ha! I knew it. Come on, Annalise, you have to take this job. You're perfect for it, and it's perfect for you."

"What about Dave? I can't ask him to move again."

"Why not?"

"His business."

"He's about to lose his business, remember?"

"We don't know that."

"Okay, he has cancer and he won't be able to work soon anyway."

"We don't know that either."

"Okay, there's another woman, and you must relocate him as far away as possible so as to avoid temptation."

Her breath hitched in her throat, stopping the French fries on their way down dead in their tracks.

"Too soon?"

She swallowed hard, took a drink of her soda, and cringed. "A little, yes."

"Sorry."

"A lot, actually."

"Won't happen again."

Yes, it would. She could count on Zachary Leebow to be brutally honest with her, to never tread lightly on her feelings, and to call her out when she was in denial. And, for that, she was grateful.

"If Dave agrees to move, it isn't you forcing him. He isn't a child."

Ouch. "I suppose that's true, but I just asked him to leave a city where he was happy and his business was doing well. For me."

"You're worth it."

Heat rose into her cheeks. She dipped her head. "Thanks, but that isn't the point. What if he's made enough sacrifices for my career already?" She thought her last job in Memphis was "the one." What if she didn't truly know what she wanted? What if she never found satisfaction in a job? What if Dave got tired of following her around?

"Stop it." Zach wadded his hamburger paper into a tight ball.

"What?"

"Thinking all the worst what-ifs. If Dave loves you and wants what's best for you, moving for your job won't be a burden, it will be an honor."

"Where on earth did you learn all this, Mr. Forever Single?"

His eyes widened, and he cocked a lopsided grin. "You forget how observant I am. And intelligent. And handsome."

A laugh burst out. "Yes, I'm so sorry. I have forgotten." She paused. "I've missed this, Zach."

"Me too. But seriously, Lise, ignoring your fears and problems won't make them go away. It will just drive wedges between you, like my mom and...never mind." He jerked to his feet. "Just tell Dave how you feel and that you're taking the job."

"Yes, boss." Except that she couldn't.

Chapter Six

"When's Dave gonna be home?" Zach, leaning against her kitchen counter, munched on some pretzels.

"Do you ever stop eating?"

"Nope. You know this about me, and you still love me." He winked.

She giggled and sank into a kitchen chair with her coffee in hand. The drive to Nashville and back had taken more out of her than she would like to admit. Probably wasn't the drive itself but the worry niggling in the back of her mind. She shouldn't have been surprised to come in at seven and find Dave still out, but she was. Some part of her had hoped her fears were imagined and that he would greet her at the door with a kiss like the old days.

"Earth to Annalise."

"I don't know." Three little words, snappier than she intended. "Sorry."

"No worries. You up for looking at my map?"

"Map?"

"Yeah, that's what I needed your help with."

"I completely forgot. But, yeah. What do you have?"

He pulled a laminated piece of paper, sealed in a small, clear evidence bag, from his pocket and handed it to her.

"Definitely a portion of a trail map. Hang on." She grabbed two three-inch binders from the bookshelf in the den and returned. "Here."

"That all trail maps?"

"Yep. Been collecting them over the years. This one is Smokies only, so we should probably start there."

He took the chartreuse one and leafed through. "This may take all night."

She smiled. "More coffee?"

"Please. And snacks."

She rolled her eyes. "I should have known."

Three hours later, they had eliminated only about a third of the trail maps. She yawned, and Zach matched it with one of his own.

"I'm too tired to drive you home, Zach. Why don't you just borrow my car? I'm off tomorrow, and you can bring it back after your shift."

"Sure."

"Your last day as a regular old officer, eh?"

"Yep. Should be yours too."

"I'll think about it. Here." She handed him the keys and hugged him briefly. "Be safe."

"Keep this." He shoved the map piece into her hand. "See what you can come up with for me, please?"

"Of course. You know I love puzzles." She didn't walk him out. There was no need. They'd known each other far too long to need to do those kinds of guestly things. She carried her mug to the sink and washed it.

The front door swung open again.

Seated at Annalise's feet, Millie lifted her head. Her ears perked, but she didn't make a move to rise.

"You forget something?"

"I live here." Dave's deep voice sounded from the living room.

"Oh, hey, hon. I'm in the kitchen."

He clomped through the house and stopped in the doorway, leaning against the frame and crossing his arms over his chest.

"You're home late." She hoped the smile she had forced made her tone as light as it should be. A joke. Not a worry.

"How long has Zach been here?"

Seriously? Why did it matter? "We drove to Nashville for work today. Then worked on something for one of his cases."

"So you've been together all day."

It wasn't a question or a statement. More an accusation. Of what, she wasn't certain. She moved to the table before she answered. Stalling for the right words, the right tone that wouldn't zing his head clear off.

Millie followed and plopped down, her head resting over Annalise's left shoe. "Yeah. Since when are you jealous of Zach?"

"I'm not." He kissed her on the forehead as he brushed past. "I'm going to bed."

He'd never had a problem with Zach before, had he? Why all of a sudden now? She dropped her head to the table and closed her eyes. This wasn't happening. It couldn't be. They had a utopian marriage in a utopian town. He'd been out late working, doing his best to provide for them. Preparing for a family in the near future, if his comments several months ago were still true and that was still his desire.

Wait.

He'd been out until ten, and he'd marched in and had the gall to act like he should be upset about Zach? Her eyes snapped open, and she lifted her head. He'd intentionally deferred the spotlight from himself. Ugh. That couldn't be a good sign. She may not be a trained interrogator, but she'd learned enough by osmosis over the years to know that tactic meant the party felt guilt over something.

Her shoulder muscles tightened, so she raised a hand to massage the most painful of the two. Her body seemed to know what her heart wasn't yet ready to admit.

Something brushed against the window, and Cody jumped, lifting his head from the math textbook he'd been slaving over for three hours. He was never going to understand pre-algebra. Never.

He paused the music playing from his laptop.

A burst of thunder crackled in the sky.

Good. It was the wind brushing the holly bush against the panes. Same noise he'd heard every storm for years.

"You dork. You're jumpy since you found that gun."

Speaking aloud let some of the pent-up anxiety out, but it didn't really exhaust the never-ending supply.

He should never have listened to Paul and Braden. The gun spelled trouble from the moment they'd lifted it from that dude's campsite. Good thing he'd gotten rid of it before Braden could talk him into any more brilliant ideas.

His phone beeped, and he retrieved it from his desk.

"You coming or what?"

He typed a quick reply. "Yeah."

His mom working a rotating shift had one big benefit. There was no one to stop him sneaking out after dark on a school night. If she wasn't at work, she was sleeping and getting ready to go back. In this Podunk town, where nothing ever happened, what she would be keeping him from was a mystery anyway.

Braden waited at the corner next to the library with four rolls of toilet paper and a broad grin.

Cody rolled his eyes. "Really, Bray? TPing again?"

"Nothin' else to do."

That was true. "All right, who's next?"

"Coach Huntley."

Cody chuckled. Nobody liked Coach Huntley. As good a target as anyone. Sometimes it paid to live in the same town as all their teachers.

Other times not so much. Like last summer when his dad made him mow every one of their yards because he'd gotten detention on the last day for being disrespectful. Whatever. His dad had said his punishment would teach him better manners. All it really taught him was where everyone lived, for moments like this.

"You ever find your dad's credit card?"

Cody shook his head. He'd lifted it from his dad's wallet six months ago, before Dad had moved out. Never used it, but Braden didn't need to know that. Just having it in his possession was enough to make Cody feel like the world was at his fingertips.

But he'd lost it somewhere on his and Braden's big weekend in Gatlinburg. Oh, well. If someone found it and started running up the amount, it'd serve his dad right for leaving his mom.

They started down the nicely lit and well-manicured sidewalk farther into this particular cul-de-sac neighborhood. Cody took a roll of toilet paper Braden offered, but he couldn't shake the feeling someone was following them. *Dork. Grow up, will ya?*

Chapter Seven

It was seventy-eight degrees by eleven a.m. Unusually hot for early October, just like the sweltering summer had been. But the perfect day to call it his last as a Gatlinburg Police Department officer. Not that he hadn't liked his job. He had. But Zach was ready for whatever God had planned next.

Including calling it off with Jo. When she got home Monday. That kind of thing shouldn't be texted or done over the phone.

He walked into the police department and stopped under the air conditioning vent. Ah, that felt good.

"Hey, Zach. Congratulations," one of the other officers said as he passed.

"Thanks, man."

He swung into the breakroom for a cup of coffee. A banner above his head read, "Congratulations!"

And a cookie cake on the table said, "We will miss you, Officer Leebow."

He hadn't expected any kind of goodbye. Was he making a mistake leaving the friends he'd made here? He shook his head. Nah. No looking back. With a corner of the cookie cake in one hand and coffee in the other, he was stopped by Captain Smith just short of his desk.

"Get on down to the ME's office, Zach. Got some info for you."

"Yes, sir."

"Oh, and hey, this case will be transferred to your new task force as of today. Congratulations. You all have your first case."

Zach thrust his shoulders back. "Thank you, sir." If only he had Annalise on board with a definitive yes. Maybe this case would be her tipping point. If it weren't for that jerk of a husband, she'd have jumped on the opportunity.

He drove the forty-five minutes to the Knoxville office and entered the front. "I believe Doc's waiting for me?"

"Hey, Zach," Andrea said from behind the receptionist's desk. "You can head on back. He'll be happy you're finally here."

"Why? Something exciting?"

"Must be. He's all worked up."

Zach's pulse spiked as he made his way down the long hallway and through the metal door. "Hey, Doc."

"Zach, so glad to see you. Come," he waved his hand, "see what I've found."

Zach leaned over the body and looked where Doc pointed.

"The bullet entered here, exited in back. It's from a .357. The bullet burst into too many fragments to try to match striations, and I suspect there may have been more fragments at the scene."

If they could find the campsite, maybe there would be more evidence. It seemed like a long shot.

"See this tattoo?" Doc lifted the man's arm to reveal an odd marking over the man's left ribs.

"Yeah. What is that?"

"It's the mark of the Moonshine Mafia."

A chortle escaped his lips. "You've got to be kidding me."

"I'm deadly serious."

"How have I not heard about them?"

"They have been dormant—or at least we thought they were—for more than half a decade."

"Okay…"

"This is a fantastic clue as to the man's identity, young Zachary. The Moonshine Mafia was led by a man named Jimmy Vern Buchanan."

"You're joking, aren't you? Pulling my chain?"

"I'm really not. He went to prison on a variety of charges but was released on probation last year."

Zach shook his head. "They couldn't have come up with a better name? It sounds like a cartoon."

Doc shrugged. "The point is, if this victim has this particular tattoo, he is linked to Mr. Buchanan."

Doc chuckled. "Though I would use the gentlemanly term 'mister' loosely where he is concerned."

"Thanks, Doc. This is a great start."

"One more thing. I found this in his pocket." Doc held up a small, plastic, black-capped tube.

"A water filter."

"Yep."

The man was most likely a backpacker then. He needed to get back to Annalise's and figure out which map section he'd found.

A knock on the front door woke Annalise. How was it already noon? Sleep had not come easily last night, but the last time she'd slept past eight was during her teenage years. "Just a minute!"

Dave hadn't kissed her goodbye this morning like he always had. His whiskery chin always stirred her awake, and she hadn't felt his light peck on her forehead. Actually, she couldn't remember him kissing her goodbye in the last several days. Or weeks. How long had it been? And why was she just now noticing?

Her phone beeped with a message.

"Get up, lazy bones. I've got news."

Figured. She rolled her eyes but smiled. Maybe Zach would have a bagel and coffee? "Key is under the frog thingy. I'll be out in a minute. Did ya bring me breakfast?"

"Nope."

She chuckled. Oh well. She threw on some sweat pants and a clean t-shirt and padded into the living room.

Zach held out a Panera bread bag and cup.

"Thought you didn't bring me breakfast."

"I didn't. Brought you lunch."

His crooked smile made her laugh. "Fine. So I slept all day. What's your point?"

"No point. Here."

She took the bag and inhaled the sweetness of a cinnamon bagel. "Mmm. Thank you."

"Your favorite."

"My favorite." She took a sip of coffee and sighed again. "What's up?"

"Coroner found a strange tattoo of a little whiskey bottle on the dead man. Believes he's part of the Moonshine Mafia. Ever heard of 'em?"

"Seems like I remember something. Not sure though."

"And a water filter. You know, the Sawyer ones."

"Yeah, I have one myself. So, the guy was maybe backpacking."

"More than likely."

"And if we can get this piece of map to fit, we'll know where to begin."

"We?"

"Huh?"

"You said we. Does that mean you're taking the job?"

She had said we, hadn't she? "I don't know."

"Campsites near Little Pigeon."

"Yeah, I've narrowed it down a bit. And I think I've found a match." She opened the book to a map of trails and backcountry sites located near Elkmont.

Zach leaned in. "Hey, look at that. Good job, Annalise."

"Thanks."

"Let's go."

She wrinkled her brow. "Right now?"

"Sure."

"I can't today."

"Yeah, neither can I."

She laughed. "Why did you suggest it then?"

He shrugged. "This weekend then."

"Deal."

"The case is transferring to SMIF. By Saturday it will be their—our—jurisdiction."

"You really should stop calling it SMIF."

"Probably should. You have two days to let them know if you're in or out."

She chewed on her cheek "I know. I don't need you to remind me, Zach."

"Well, either way we can hike out on our own time. Right?"

"True." She smiled.

He spun on his heels and headed for the front door. "Here's your keys." He tossed them over his shoulder.

Somehow she caught them. "How are you getting back to work?"

"Walking."

"Okay." Wait, what? "You can't walk! It's like forty-five miles." But he was already out the front door. She trotted after him, swung the door open, and peered down the street. Her car was parked in her driveway, and a police cruiser shot away, with Zach in the passenger seat. She giggled. What a goofball. A loveable, sweet goofball. *Thank you for Zach's friendship, Lord.* She had a feeling she was going to need it more than ever soon.

Chapter Eight

At least working still felt normal. Annalise settled into her cruiser's seat and sighed. No, it didn't. Nothing felt normal. Nothing felt right when her and Dave's relationship was so wrong. She had to pin her husband down and talk to him. Why was that so hard for her?

Because she was afraid of what he would say.

She sighed. It was going to be a long night.

After a full city patrol—twice— then driving through to get dinner at Wendy's, and circling back over Norris Dam, Annalise's mind still would not rest. She texted Dave. "I miss you. Can we meet up and talk?"

And then held her breath. When had she last told him that she missed him? Ugh. She hadn't exactly been lovey-dovey lately. She'd blame it on the stress of the job, if she could. But that would be dishonest.

Her radio crackled to life. "Officer Baker, please respond to 152 Lee Lane. Non-emergency. Complaints of vandalism."

Annalise rolled her eyes. Vandalism in this little town meant toilet paper in trees. "Ten-four. ETA five minutes."

She pulled into Coach Huntley's driveway and pushed down a smile. How many times had she responded to this gruff older man's house for TPing? The students must hate him. As soon as she stepped from the vehicle, Coach Huntley stormed down the driveway.

"I caught them on video this time, Officer Baker. I know exactly who it is, and I want them brought to justice."

Justice? For toilet papering? "Yes, sir. I understand how upsetting this must be for you. Can you show me the video, please?"

She followed him inside, where he replayed a clip from the night prior on his computer. Two boys sneaked into his yard around midnight and proceeded to unwrap, unroll, and cover every reachable surface with the white, flowery-stitched paper. "Do you know their names?"

"Absolutely. Cody Moss and Braden Seeber. Eighth grade. Couple of hooligans who are in detention every other week."

"I will get their addresses and go speak with their parents."

"I want them to clean this mess up, Officer." Coach Huntley gritted his teeth. "That little delinquent. After I tipped him extra for mowing my lawn last summer and everything."

"I will keep you updated, sir. Please refrain from contacting the students and parents yourself. This is now a police matter." Police matter? For toilet papering. This was the town she lived in and loved, but really?

Zach had a murder that needed solving and required hiking into the mountains she loved even more. It required real investigation and would, hopefully, bring healing and closure to a grieving family and justice to a murderer.

Maybe she should take the job. Dave would support her like always. He would recognize how much she needed the challenges the new task force would bring. How much she loved being involved in the cases that made a real difference in people's lives. Wouldn't he?

Her phone beeped with an incoming message from Dave.

"I can do a late lunch."

She sighed and replied. "I'm sorry, just got a call. Can we talk at dinner?"

"Big surprise."

Annalise frowned. He knew she had to do her job. It wasn't her fault she'd caught a call. Why was he being so huffy? "I love you. I promise I'll come home at dinnertime and we can spend time together."

"Don't know if I'll make it home. Working on a big job."

Tears threatened to climb to her eyes. She stuffed them down and aimed for Cody Moss's house. A knot the size of a baseball settled into her stomach. Things with Dave were worse than she thought, and she didn't even know exactly why.

Cody slammed the math book shut. Why did he even try anymore? It wasn't like he could study his way out of failing. Not with his dumb brain calling the shots. He never dreamed eighth grade would be so hard.

That's why his dad had left. He was ashamed of his no-good, lazy, stupid son. The one who could never do anything right and constantly disappointed him. His dad hadn't said it, but he hadn't needed to.

As Cody walked by, he glanced out the window, and his stomach dropped. A police cruiser slowed and pulled into the driveway. Great. Just great.

If he hurried, he could sneak out the back door and disappear between houses.

He bolted down the stairs, pausing at the bottom and listening for his mother. The doorbell rang. He jumped and backed into the hallway.

"Going somewhere?"

His mother's voice made him jump again. "Uh, yeah. Out with Braden."

"Is that doorbell for you?"

"Nah."

"Why do I get the feeling you're lying to me?"

Because he was. He shrugged.

"Don't move, young man."

He knew better than to disobey that cold, hard-toned command. As much as the police on the other side of the door freaked him out, his mother worried him more.

"Cody! Get in here. Now!" his mother hollered from the direction of the front door.

Here goes nothing. He squared his shoulders and entered the foyer. The look on the woman officer's face was anything but menacing. Was she getting ready to bust out laughing?

"Cody Moss?"

He nodded then dropped his head.

"Coach Huntley has video of you vandalizing his yard."

His mom planted her hands on her hips and scowled. "Cody Alvis Moss."

"Aw, come on, Mom. It ain't vandalism. Not like spray paint and stuff. Just toilet paper."

"Again, Son? We have talked about this."

More like she had talked and he had tried to tune her out. "What's it matter?"

"Ms. Moss," the officer piped in, "I'd like to take Cody for a little drive over to Coach Huntley's house. I'll be picking up a Braden Seeber on the way. If they do not clean up the coach's yard, he plans to press charges."

His mom gasped. "Certainly. Of course. Yes, whatever you need to do."

"Mo-om."

"Do not take that tone with me. You did this to yourself." She crossed her arms over her chest. "Sounds to me like you got lucky. If Coach Huntley wants to make this a bigger deal, he easily can."

Great. There went the rest of this evening. At least they weren't able to pin all the prior times on him. Figured Coach Huntley would get surveillance cameras. "Ugh, fine." He slammed the door behind him as he followed the lady outside.

Annalise tucked Cody into the backseat and shut the door. She finally let out the chuckle she'd been barely containing. Cody was mad, that much was obvious. He'd done something he shouldn't, and he'd gotten caught. But the fact that he still obeyed his mother meant there was hope for him yet. Right? He was still young enough to "set straight" before toilet paper turned into illegal substances or shoplifting or worse.

She slid into the driver's seat and glanced at him in the rearview. "Coach Huntley is pretty upset with you and Braden."

"Yeah. So what?"

"If he wanted to, he could press charges for vandalism."

Cody didn't respond.

"Listen, kid—"

"I ain't no kid."

Oh, yeah, right. He sounded so mature with his improper grammar and whiny tone and baby smooth skin. "Cody, you have a whole life ahead of you. This isn't exactly the best way to kick-start everything. Is it?"

"What does it matter?"

"I'm sure your mom feels differently. And what would your father say?"

"Dunno. He left." Cody turned his gaze toward the window.

Ouch. Poor kiddo. It had taken its toll on Zach when his father walked out when he was a sophomore, and Cody was two years younger. "I'm sorry to hear that."

"Don't need your pity, lady."

"Didn't say you did." She sighed. This—this rough, snotty, pre-teen boloney—was why she didn't want children. How was she supposed to diffuse the tension and let him know she wasn't some dumb grownup who didn't care? She never knew what to say to kids.

She drove the rest of the way to Braden's house and then on to Coach Huntley's, speaking as few words as possible.

Coach Huntley met them in the driveway with two garbage bags and some work gloves. And the biggest frown she'd seen yet.

While the boys cleaned, she and Coach Huntley stood in the shade of an ancient oak tree, sipping iced sweet tea.

"He's so smart, that one." Coach Huntley pointed to Cody. "Such a waste to see him failing his classes and skipping school, and apparently sneaking out in the middle of the night."

"Mm-hmm." It was a waste. Why couldn't Cody see things more clearly? His mom seemed to genuinely care. He lived in a nice town, with good schools. He had opportunities a lot of kids would kill to have.

"Too bad his dad hightailed it out last year."

"About that. I know it's none of my business, but do you know where he went or why he left?"

Coach Huntley sucked on his teeth for a moment before he crossed his arms and lowered his voice. "Rumor is, Brian Moss had another family. A secret one next state over."

"No. That only happens on television."

"Yeah. He traveled a lot for work and was keeping up with two separate lives, apparently. Poor kid has been heartbroken ever since."

"I can see why. That's enough to break a grownup's heart, let alone a kid."

He nodded. "Yep. That's why I'm not pressing charges."

"Mighty big of you."

Coach Huntley smiled smugly.

It was good he wasn't pressing charges, but wasn't there something someone could do to help Cody more? A guidance counselor or teacher maybe? She'd have to make some calls in the morning and see if she could encourage someone to reach out.

"Officer Baker, what are you doing here today?" Principal Greene greeted her.

She stopped in front of the check-in desk at Norris Middle School and smiled. "I wondered if I might speak with you about one of your students."

"Of course. Follow me."

Annalise followed Principal Greene and her pin skirt, striped blouse, and bun into the glass-paneled office. The woman was the epitome of a stereotypical middle school principal, but Annalise had always found her to be kind.

"How can I help you?"

"Cody Moss. I wouldn't want word to spread, but I picked him up for vandalism yesterday. He made some comments that led me to believe he is struggling with his father's absence."

"I believe his father travels frequently for work, yes?"

"Yes, but apparently he actually left the family last year."

Principal Greene sank into her chair. "I had no idea. No wonder his grades have been falling."

"Are there extra services available to him?"

"Yes, of course. I will pull him out of class today to meet with the guidance counselor. She can't force him to talk, but she sure can try."

"Thank you."

"I feel terrible that I've missed this."

"You have a hundred and fifty students, Mrs. Greene. The important thing is that he doesn't slip through the cracks any longer. Right?"

"Right, yes, you're right. Thank you for bringing this to my attention."

Annalise's chest swelled. Cody had potential, and she'd hate to see him throw it away. Too bad she couldn't talk some sense into the absentee jerk of a father too.

Chapter Nine

Annalise cinched her pack's waist strap tight. "Ready?"

Zach nodded. "Let's get this show on the road."

"Trail."

"Precisely."

Annalise giggled. "Lead the way, Special Agent Leebow."

"I'd rather let the professional hiker lead. After you." He bowed and motioned toward the trail with an outstretched hand. "Special Agent Baker."

"I didn't take the job. Remember? The deadline was yesterday."

"Not anymore."

She pinned him with a sharp glare. "What?"

"Changed my mind. I'll go first." He trotted up the trail, away from her, and then tossed a glance over his shoulder.

"Zachary! Get back here!"

"Not on your life, Annalise!"

She raced to catch up to him, and when she did, she found him lounging on a rock at a bend in the trail. "What are you talking about?"

"I told the team you needed a day or two more to decide."

He wasn't wrong, exactly.

"And that you'd more than likely agree."

"You what?" She smacked his biceps. But he still wasn't wrong. She sank onto the rock next to him and leaned back, folding her hands behind her head. The leaves above danced in a slight breeze, tickling the blue skyline beyond. She did want the job. Why couldn't she just say yes? Ugh. She'd already asked that question. The answer still evaded her.

"If Dave loves you, he will support you in this, Lise." He sighed. "If he's moved on, this will be a strong catalyst."

How did Zach know exactly which nail to hit on the head? She nodded, even as a tear formed in the corner of her eyes. "That's what I'm afraid of. If I don't take the job, maybe I can keep denying anything is wrong. Just keep going like everything's fine."

"Until it isn't."

"Yeah."

"One way or another, the truth will come out. Both if there is something situational going on and the true state of his heart. Do you really want to put off finding out?"

She shook her head.

"Then say yes."

"I'll think about it."

He frowned.

"I really will." She brushed at her cheeks and jumped to her feet. "Come on, we've got work to do."

The sun-splotched trail ahead called to her, as it always did. It asked her to discover what lay around the next bend, over the next hill, through the next stream. It begged her to uncover hidden beauties—the tiny wildflowers nodding their heads in the shade of the hundred-year-old trees, the spiders waiting in their woven webs between branches, the birds speaking to their feathered, flittering mates. Too bad she couldn't get lost out here and live like a native wild woman. Build a home in the middle of the dense, peaceful forest and dwell with the birds and beasts for the rest of her life. They wouldn't make her feel this way. Wouldn't give her this fear of the future imploding around her. Wouldn't love her and then stop someday.

They questioned the backcountry campers at the first two rustic sites. No one had seen someone fitting the dead man's description.

Three hours, a liter of water, and two granola bars in, they reached the remotest backcountry site and found it empty.

"Well," Zach said as he plopped onto a stump, "what next?"

"Other than finding a place to go potty, you mean?"

"Take your pick." He swung his arms wide. "Mother Nature's toilets."

"I'll be back in a minute. Stay put."

"Can't move anyway."

"You're out of shape, Leebow."

"Tell me about it."

Zach drained his bottle and wandered to the creek to filter and refill. He squatted next to the clear, babbling water, swiping another sheen of sweat from his forehead.

"Zach!" Annalise's shout raced through the trees.

"Annalise!" Where was she? He strained his ears, listening for her next call so he could pinpoint which direction to run.

"Up here!"

She waved to him from the top of a steep ascent.

"Why on earth did you go up there to…well, you know?"

"Oh, for Pete's sake, just get up here!"

He scrambled up the hillside, slipping on leaf litter and mushrooms. "How did you do that so easily?"

Annalise grinned. "I came up the trail." She pointed. "Over there."

"Oh, gee. Thanks for telling me."

"You're welcome."

He exaggerated his doubled-over panting, earning a genuine laugh. At least she was laughing. His upside-down-bug-like movements coming up the hill were worth it.

She grabbed his hand and dragged him along. "Look."

A sagging green-sided tent, two camp chairs, and a makeshift fire ring sat in the middle of a slight depression.

"This is pretty far outside the markers for the campsite."

"Yep."

His mind raced. This could be the clue he needed.

"We need to check registered campers. Of course, if these people were willing to camp outside the regulated perimeter, they probably didn't register their hiking plans either. But it's worth a shot."

"Good idea." He knelt to inspect the fire ring. Cool, rain-soaked ashes. So it hadn't been used since before the storm. He used a stick to dig through the pile but found nothing noteworthy. No slips of paper or receipts.

"Take a look at this."

Annalise held the door flap open for him to peer inside. One sleeping mat, one pillow. One pair of boots that smelled horrible. And broken glass scattered everywhere. Odd. Something had happened here. Whether it was accident or foul play, he couldn't say with certainty yet.

The wind kicked up, fluttering the sides of the tent and causing the sunlight to change. When it settled, a point of light beamed through a finger-sized hole in the back wall. "Hey, Annalise."

"Yeah?"

"Go around back for a second, please."

Her footsteps crunched around the edge of the tent.

"See what I see?"

"Huh? Oh, yeah. Bullet hole?"

"Certainly the right size."

"I'll see if I can find anything in the trees back here."

Zach took photos with his phone. The sun inside the tent shifted again, glinting off the glass scattered on the floor. What happened here? He used a pair of gloves to lift several pieces coated with dried red and slipped them into a baggy. He didn't like to make assumptions, but it seemed a fairly safe bet it was blood.

Under the edge of the sleeping mat, he extracted several pieces of cracked corn. Why on earth would someone hike with cracked corn? Unless he had a poacher on his hands. Maybe the dead man had sneaked back here in order to set up deer baits. Or bear.

But how had that gotten him killed?

And why was there no sleeping bag? Not even a blanket.

Annalise returned and hovered at the opening of the tent. "Nothing."

He turned and smiled. "Okay, thanks for checking." The sun framed Annalise's already golden head, setting her aglow. His breath caught. Wow. His best friend was gorgeous.

"What?"

"Nothin'."

"Quit being weird, Zach." Annalise disappeared.

He chuckled. But maybe it wasn't so funny. She was a married woman, his soon-to-be teammate, and his longest and dearest friend. The strange new thoughts weren't coming from a place of attraction, but rather concern and platonic love. They had to be. She was like a little sister. An annoying little sister. He nodded, closing the door and dead-bolting it on those thoughts.

On the way out, they stopped at the closest ranger station and requested a printout of all recent backcountry campers. Annalise headed for home, and he headed for the Gatlinburg Police Station. Until the new SMIF—

He chuckled. SMIF, terrible acronym

—headquarters was prepared, he needed a place to run these names.

"Hello, sir," he greeted his prior captain. "Do you mind if I use a computer?"

"Sure, Leebow. Just close it down when you finish and lock the door when you leave. The night crew is out on patrol."

"Thank you, sir."

With a bag of honey-roasted peanuts and a Mountain Dew, he dove into the long list of names.

They'd given him every backcountry camper in the park, but he started with the ones specifically listed near the Little Pigeon. He cut the names by approximately thirty percent by simply marking off all the definitely female names.

But two hours later, he'd run all the names, even the ones from parts of the park nowhere near the Little Pigeon, and come up empty. None of the driver's license photos matched their dead man. And he was back to square one.

Chapter Ten

Annalise's eyelids fluttered open to a dark room. She rolled over and squinted. The sky was still black too. What time was it? And why was she awake?

Dave wasn't in bed. And his side was cold.

Where on earth was he? She held her breath and listened. His deep voice muttered through the walls from the direction of the kitchen.

With her throat so tight she could scarcely breathe, she slipped on her robe and crept down the hallway, pausing just outside the kitchen.

"I have to go. I'll see you soon." His voice was low, intentionally quiet, as if he tried not to wake her.

Silence spanned for more than a minute, then the sounds of water running and the smell of coffee brewing met her. She sighed and rolled her eyes. Of course he was trying to be quiet, it was early. He wasn't sneaking, just being respectful.

"Morning, hon," she said as she stepped through the doorway.

Dave dropped the coffee creamer, spilling its milky contents over a large section of the green and gray tile. "Sheesh, you scared the daylights out of me."

"No daylights yet." She grinned.

He looked up with a frown on his face. "Huh?"

"It's dark. No day lights."

"Oh."

Well, that joke could only have fallen flatter if it were actually part of the floor. "What's up?"

"Huh?"

"Why are you up so early?"

"Oh, um, got to get to a work site that is quite a drive away. Out toward Gatlinburg."

She sighed. There really was a job. *Thank you, Lord!* "Maybe you'll run into Zach." As soon as the words left her mouth, she wished she could grab them and cram them back in.

Dave sent her a look she wasn't used to seeing on his face.

So, he was still upset about the other day. But why? "You know he and I are just friends. Right? Like we always have been?"

"Yeah." He shrugged.

"Want to ride together?"

"No."

She raised her eyebrow.

"Sorry. It's just I have to take the work truck so I have my tools and equipment and stuff."

A heavy, burning sensation stirred to life in her stomach. He'd answered so quickly. "Oh, right. Of course."

She grabbed a wet rag, then stooped to help him sop up the mess. "We never had that talk, you know."

He didn't turn toward her.

She took a deep breath. "I have a job offer."

His face flushed a darker shade.

"In the Gatlinburg area, actually." She giggled nervously.

"With Zach?"

She hesitated.

"Of course it is."

"Dave." She reached for his arm, but he pulled it from her grasp. "What's really going on? You've never had any issues with Zach before. Why all of a sudden now?"

He scrubbed the already-cleaned floor a bit harder.

"Are we…are we okay?" She wasn't ready for his answer.

He opened his mouth, closed it again. Then pressed his lips together.

Her phone rang. Oh, perfect timing. "I love you, Dave." She didn't wait to see if he answered this time. Instead she swiped at a tear and answered, leaving him alone in the kitchen.

"We need you to come in, Annalise." Her captain's grainy voice sounded heavy with fatigue, like he hadn't had his first pot of coffee yet.

"Yes, sir. What's wrong?"

"We have a missing teen."

Her heart sank. One of their town kids was missing? How? "Who?"

He ruffled through papers. "Cody Moss."

No! She placed a hand over her heart, willing it to keep working properly. "Runaway?"

"We don't believe so." He sighed, and Annalise could picture his stout fingers rubbing the furrowed brow, the frown on his face. The genuine concern for one of his citizens.

"Just come in, Baker. I'll explain everything."

Poor Cody! Poor Ms. Moss! Maybe it wasn't as bad as it seemed. Cody was rebelling, angry that his father had left. Surely he was just out late protesting his punishment from Coach Huntley. Her hands shook as she strapped her utility belt around her waist.

Dave was gone when she entered the kitchen to tell him goodbye. *Lord, I don't know what to do. With any of this.*

Had she remembered to pray about the situation with Dave yet? *Sorry, Lord. I always do that, don't I?* Rushing ahead and not waiting for instructions. Trying to fix everything before she needed Him to intervene. If she could find the answers, she wouldn't have to bother Him.

Maybe the whole thing with Cody would be one of those resolved-by-lunch, found-him-smoking-in-the-school-yard kind of problems.

The sun pierced the sky in a shaft of brilliant red as she pulled into the station. Every light shone. Every officer's squad car waited in the open bay or drive. A canine officer whipped in behind her. Oh, no. That wasn't a promising sign.

She entered the station and found her fellow officers huddled in the bay, Captain Brooks on the phone nearby, and a table with fresh coffee and bagels. They must have been planning for a long morning. Not a good sign either.

"Baker, good. I see you were the one who ran the call for vandalism involving the missing boy. Can you tell us anything about him?"

Annalise cleared her throat as the room grew quiet. "He seemed like a sweet kid, but he was troubled. His dad left sometime last year, and it seemed to have hit Cody hard."

"Do you think he could have run away?"

She bit her cheek and released it. "It's a possibility, yes."

"All right. Hopefully the dogs will give us a good lead, then."

She stepped to the back of the group and waited for instructions. Cody was missing. Missing. The boy she'd gotten frustrated with over being a kid. How could she have called him snotty? Granted, it was in her head. But still.

They were going to find him. He had simply snuck out again and not come back before his mom noticed. Simple. He was probably out throwing toilet paper over more trees and lost track of time.

"Captain?"

"Yes, Officer Baker?"

"We may need to check houses that have any evidence of toilet papering in the yard. That seems to be Cody's and his friend's MO."

Some of the men chuckled.

"Good idea. Brown and Stinson. Patrol the town and look for TPd trees. Annalise, you go to Cody's house and speak with his mother. Start processing the scene."

Scene? Was there something he wasn't telling her?

"It could still be a runaway, and we need to cover all bases, but...well, you'll see for yourself when you get there."

Annalise nodded. That couldn't be good either.

"The canine team will be there momentarily."

Lord, please don't let us need them. Have Cody show up by the time I get there.

Cody wanted to scream, but fear trapped his voice. If it wasn't so dark, he wouldn't be so scared. If he could just see that no one was standing in front of him with a gun or knife, ready to plunge it into his throat, he could breathe again. If he could just sit up and stretch out, make sure he wasn't buried alive, he could stop the pounding of his heart. He squirmed. It was pointless. His shoulder sockets screamed for him, his nerve endings and brain the only recipients of their pain. Where was he? Why was it so hard to move?

His mother would know by now that he wasn't in his room. Wouldn't she? It had been hours since his abduction. Hadn't it?

His mother. She'd be worried sick. He had to get home and tell her he was okay. A tear wetted his face, sliding down his cheek and plopping somewhere into the darkness.

How long could a person go in total black before they went blind? He remembered hearing about it when they went to The Lost Sea. He was, what, seven years old? His dad had bought him that sack of dirt and let him find all the gemstones in the fake mine washing station thingy. And then ice cream at the Mayfield farm. His mom and dad had laughed and smiled and treated him like he was the best thing in the world. His dad...

Would they call him too?

What if they thought he'd run away? It could take them days to even begin a search, and by then, who knew what would be left of Cody Moss, the dork afraid of the dark and shadows.

Chapter Eleven

Celine Moss hugged her knees and rocked on the front steps of her house when Annalise approached. The officer that had been waiting with her scooched to the curb and nodded at her. The look on his face said he was happy to put some distance between himself and the panicked mother.

"Ms. Moss?"

She turned reddened, tear-filled eyes toward Annalise. "Officer Baker. Oh, I'm so glad to see you." Celine rushed her and wrapped her arms around Annalise's waist. "You have to find my boy. You have to…"

Annalise gently backed away with her heart in her throat. "We are going to do our best." The words were almost too large for her to squeak out. "I need you to tell me everything you know."

"I…I don't know anything. That's the problem." Celine melted into a sobbing puddle on the top step again.

"When did you first notice Cody was missing?"

"I went to tell him I was leaving for work, around four a.m., like I always do when I work mornings. And his bed was empty." She hiccupped. "At first I thought he had snuck out again. But I called everyone. I mean everyone. And no one has seen him."

"Is there a chance Cody ran away?"

Celine shook her head. "Well, yes. He has been such a mess since his dad left. I have too, really. But no, not this time."

"Why not, ma'am?"

"Come on. I'll show you."

Her feet felt heavy as she followed Cody's mom inside and up the stairs. Celine pushed open the bedroom door and motioned for Annalise to step through.

"Your captain said he'd have the forensics—" Celine clamped a hand to her mouth.

Annalise put a gentle hand on Celine's shoulder. She urged her voice to be soothing. "I'm sorry, I can't imagine how difficult this must be for you. I need to take a look around. Okay?"

Celine nodded.

"Why don't you go downstairs and make a cup of tea?" Annalise patted Celine's trembling shoulder.

"Okay."

Annalise took in the scope of the damage to the room. There had no doubt been a struggle. By the looks of it, Cody had at least put up a good fight. A pre-algebra textbook lay open on the floor. A shade-less lamp toppled over the edge of the desk. And a pane in the window had been busted, with the glass shards splayed toward the inside. Cody hadn't broken out. Someone had broken in.

She knelt over the pieces, noticing a few droplets of blood. If they were lucky, the kidnapper had cut himself and they'd be able to get DNA. If they were really, really lucky, the DNA would match someone already in the system. After she finished taking Ms. Moss's statement, she would get the evidence kit from her car and get busy.

She returned to the kitchen and took the hot mug Celine offered. "Thank you. I hate to ask, but I have a few more questions. If you can, it would be very helpful. As I'm sure you know, at times like this, time is of the essence."

Celine sank onto a barstool, staring at the cup in her hand.

"Is Cody's dad a custodial parent?"

"Humph. Supposed to be."

"Have you notified him of the situation?"

"Not yet. I mean, I tried, but he didn't answer. He, um, he doesn't usually answer when I call. Probably afraid the new wife will be suspicious of who is on the phone." She let out a hoarse chuckle. "You know he hasn't checked on Cody in over a month?"

"I'm sorry to hear that, ma'am. If you would like for us to continue to try to reach him, we will need his contact information." It was worded as a request, but if Celine didn't willingly provide the number, Annalise would have to find it and contact him, no matter what. "Can you think of any reason someone would do this?"

"No. Neither Brian nor I have anything much of value. No big bank accounts or anything."

"It sounds horrible, but hopefully we will get a ransom call. Then there will be motivation and a way to make contact with the kidnapper. You need to stay next to the phone. We will have an officer here and set up equipment to record any calls you may receive." Annalise made some notes on her pad. "But do not step foot in Cody's room until I finish collecting evidence. Please."

Tears pooled in the corners of Celine's eyes, but she managed to nod.

"The struggle must've been pretty loud. Why didn't you hear it?"

"I have trouble sleeping. My schedule is so strange, you know. So I have a noise machine. And I usually take a Benadryl." She swallowed hard. "This is my fault. If I had been awake, if I had heard—"

"Ms. Moss, that is not what I was implying at all. I need you to stay as calm as possible."

"You don't understand what this feels like. My child—my baby—is out there somewhere, and there isn't a thing I can do about it."

"I'm sorry. You're right. I can't relate to how you feel. But I can do my job. And the next step is to get the information in for the Amber Alert. What do you think Cody was wearing? I will need a photo of him as well." She glanced at her watch. "If we hustle, we can make the six o'clock news."

Zach choked on the last swig of coffee, almost spitting it onto the television screen where Annalise stood in front of a charming home, camera lights boldly illuminating her concern-etched face.

"If you see this boy," she held up a photo and the camera zoomed in on it, "please call 9-1-1. Please do not approach him directly." She cleared her throat. "He was last seen at his home in Norris last night wearing a pair of flannel pajama bottoms and a blue t-shirt."

The camera swung to the news anchor. "Cody Moss is a Caucasian, thirteen-year-old boy, five feet six inches tall, dark brown hair, green eyes. If you have any information that could help locate him, please call 865-771-5246 immediately."

A disappearance in Annalise's little town? She would be a mess of emotions. Though she would pretend she wasn't.

He dialed Kirk. "Hey, man, I need to reschedule our pow-wow for after lunch."

"Sure thing. Anything wrong?"

"Yeah, maybe. Annalise has a new case, and I want to go make sure she doesn't need a helping hand."

"Ah, okay. Tell her I said hi and am still waiting for her yes."

"Now might not be the time. But I'll try."

He hung up with the third member of SMIF and got dressed. The big guys had recruited Kirk from the FBI field office in Knoxville because he had experience not only with investigations and missing persons but also had hiked the entire Appalachian Trail before he turned thirty-five. He was the perfect man to lead their team into this uncharted new territory.

An hour later, Zach zipped off the interstate at the Clinton exit and swung a right. Once he turned onto the road into the small town of Norris, he whistled low. The usually empty sidewalks, save for a few joggers or dog walkers, were crowded with pedestrians all headed the same direction—toward town square.

He found Annalise's captain fielding a throng of people in front of the post office. What exactly was going on here? He fought through the crowd and shook Captain Brooks's hand. "How can I help?"

Milton flashed him a half-hearted smile. "Crowd control. Biggest problem right now."

"What do they want?"

"To help look."

"Commendable."

"We intentionally left out details." Milton raised his left eyebrow. "If you get my drift."

"I do. No point in them combing the town, eh?"

"We don't believe so at this point."

"Recovery?"

"Kidnapping."

Wow. That hadn't ever happened here, had it? Not that he knew about.

A news van pulled into the parking lot, inching its way through the people.

As soon as it stopped, Zach climbed over the hood and clambered onto the roof. "Got a bullhorn, Captain?"

Milton tossed one up to him.

"People, may I have your attention please?"

The crowd slowly quieted.

"We appreciate your desire to help, but at this time, more people out looking will only confuse the dogs." He glanced toward Milton. He hadn't verified there were any dogs. The captain nodded. "Please return home and do not interfere with our investigation."

Several people booed.

"We understand your need to be involved, we really do. But this is a delicate matter. Prayers are much appreciated for the officers working this case, but, most importantly, for the boy's family and for his safe return. Thank you."

It took another twenty minutes for the crowd to actually do what he requested, and even then a few stragglers stayed behind.

"Was I not clear enough?"

Milton clapped him on the shoulder. "You were. They are concerned. This is their town, and one of them is missing. A child, no less."

That was true. Zach didn't really know what it was like to be part of such a tight-knit community. Gatlinburg wasn't a huge town by any means, but it was much larger than Norris. And touristy, so there was a much higher crime rate and fewer steady locals.

"Thanks for your help."

"Sure. Where's Annalise?"

"Headed that way myself. Come on."

Chapter Twelve

Annalise scooped up the last piece of glass and dropped it into the baggy. It had taken forever to pick each sliver from the carpet, but she was glad she had been blessed with the gift of attention to detail. The dozen or so that had blood on them would be crucial pieces to the puzzle. Hopefully.

Was Celine still on the same stool in the kitchen, alternating her stares between the phone and the emptiness of her home?

Zach appeared in the bedroom doorway. "Hey."

A half-hearted grin touched her lips. "What are you doing here?"

"Ah, just passing through."

"Just passing through, huh? You live a half hour from here."

He shrugged. "Thought you could use a hand." He opened his arms. "Or a hug?"

She shouldn't hug him. Not with the way Dave was currently feeling about their friendship, but he was right that she could use one. "How about help collecting?"

"Where do you want me to start?"

"Bed, please." She smiled. "Thanks for coming, Zach."

"Of course."

She handed him some gloves and they worked in tandem, her scouring the floor for anything else important and him picking up every hair he could locate. For the millionth time, the same questions rotated in her mind. Why had someone done this? Why Cody specifically? What did they want? How did they know where Cody was? Had they followed him? Had they watched for a prolonged period of time? Ugh. On and on the internal monologue went. Her head ached by the time she finished with the room.

With Zach's help, she had a sizeable bag of evidence for the lab. *Lord, please help it give us some answers.*

Downstairs, they found Captain Brooks talking to Celine. Instead of tears, her face now held an expressionless quality. The glassy stare she cast on the room made Annalise shiver.

"Still no word from Cody's father?" Captain Brooks asked.

Annalise shook her head.

Celine snapped to attention and drew her hands quickly to her mouth. "I don't want Brian to learn about this from the news—"

Captain Brooks patted her hand. "I'm sorry, Ms. Moss. That would be a terrible way to learn about the situation, but if that's what it takes to reach him, so be it."

Something about his tone seemed to calm Celine. She nodded and sank back onto the barstool.

Zach followed Annalise to her patrol car, where she put the evidence in the trunk and locked it up.

Zach held a somber expression that Annalise equated with deep thought. "What is it?"

"I was just thinking, y'all can't locate the father, right?"

Annalise shook her head.

"What if he decided he didn't like sharing custody and took off with the boy?"

"I thought about that. I think it is a good lead to follow."

"All right then. Good." He smiled. "Hey, I've got a meeting with Kirk. I need to get back."

"Thanks again for your help."

"Not a problem. Kirk says hi. And that he is waiting on your yes."

Annalise chuckled, but disappointment filled her. She couldn't leave NPD now, not with Cody missing. It seemed, maybe, this door wasn't one she was truly meant to walk through. Dave should be happy about that. "I need to finish this case, Zach. I can't just leave Cody's mom like this. And Milton…"

"I know. Wouldn't expect you to. But I'm willing to bet Kirk and I can handle this first case alone."

Her eyebrows arched. "What case?"

"The body in the Little Pigeon. Captain is turning jurisdiction over to us."

"Oh, good."

"I know you're meant to take this job, Annalise. I'm just waiting on you to know it too."

"Annalise?" Dave spoke from somewhere behind her.

She spun. "Hey. What's wrong?" Why was he here? Wasn't he working far away today?

"I saw on the news. Thought you might be taking things a bit personally and need some support."

Her heart melted. There was the Dave she knew. The one who could read her without even needing to be in the room. The one who cared enough to go out of his way to show her how much. She took a step toward him, arms outstretched. "You're absolutely right. This stinks."

He backed away from her. "I see you've already got Zach. Guess you don't need me so much, eh?"

"What?"

"I'll just get back to work then."

"Dave, I—"

"It's fine, Annalise. You haven't needed me in a long time. I'm pretty used to it by now."

He stomped back to his work truck and slammed the door.

Hot tears stung her eyes. This was all she needed right now. She had work to do. A tough case to focus on and her marriage was falling apart. Just perfect. What was Dave talking about? Of course she needed him. He was her husband. Zach's tender hand on her shoulder released the tears.

It was a good thing for Dave that Zach knew how much punching him in his fat nose would upset her. His insides quaked from the exertion of holding himself back. The words on his tongue would only antagonize her more, so he held them back too. But one day soon, if he had his way, those words would spill, and Annalise would know what an idiot Dave was.

"You gonna be okay if I go?"

Annalise nodded without turning to face him.

He knew she was crying. How he longed to pull her into an embrace, but that wouldn't help much either, what with Dave still able to see them in his rearview. "I can stay if you need me to."

She swiped her hands across her cheeks. "No, you go. I'll be fine. We've both got work to do."

"I'll check on you later." He hated leaving, but Kirk was waiting, and if he knew his Annalise, at a moment like this, she wanted to be alone anyway.

It took the entire hour and a half drive for his blood to stop boiling. Maybe he should reach out to Dave himself. A little man-to-man talk where Zach reminded him just what a precious woman he had by his side. He chuckled. Right. Like Annalise wouldn't kill him for that.

Kirk waited at a corner table in the dimly lit, buttery-scented Cracker Barrel.

Zach forced a smile as he slid into the seat across from him.

"You hungry?"

Zach raised his eyebrow.

Kirk laughed. "Right. Almost forgot. Well, eat up. We are headed out to that campsite you and Annalise found."

"Oh, okay. How come?"

"Results came back on the bloody glass you found. Positive match for John Doe."

He knew it. He leaned back into his chair. "We need to look for more evidence?"

"With a fine-toothed comb. You and Annalise more than likely found the murder scene."

Hopefully, no one had disturbed the campsite. He'd strung caution tape around the trees, but in hindsight that may have been a terrible idea. It was like a giant red button waiting for some unwitting passerby to want to see why exactly that spot was forbidden.

Not to mention bears. Even if there was just the faintest hint of a food smell, a bear could destroy what evidence might remain. He bounced his knee under the table as they placed their orders. Their bodies needed the fuel, but he'd almost rather just grab some protein bars and hit the trail.

"How's Annalise holding up?" Kirk asked between bites.

Rough. Zack ducked his head. Her home life was falling apart, and there wasn't a thing he could do to protect her from the pain. But he couldn't divulge details.

"That good, huh?"

Zach nodded. "It's complicated."

"I saw the rerun on the nine o'clock news. Did she know the victim?"

"She knows everyone in her little town."

"Good point. Still think she'll get on this bandwagon sometime soon?"

Zach wrinkled his brow and thought hard before responding. "I do. Something's telling me she will still say yes. But she'll have to find the boy first."

"That could take years."

Zach knew Kirk was right, but the words still stung. Who knew what the case really was at its root? It could take years to discover the true depths. To find the kidnapper. To find a body. How many missing persons cases were actually solved? He couldn't remember the exact number, but with children, the rate dropped astronomically after the first forty-eight hours. *Lord, help Annalise. Give her wisdom, stamina, and direction.*

"Ready?"

Zach chomped his last bite of burger. "Yep."

A short drive later, he was following Kirk up the trail. He'd agreed to carry the backpack full of evidence-collecting tools and bottled waters because Kirk lugged the metal detector. If he could find that bullet, the one that tore a hole through the tent, it could be a huge lead.

They reached the campsite a few hours later. Other than a few windblown leaves and a large branch that hadn't been there prior, the site appeared the same. Good.

He started with the metal detector, making careful, sweeping passes in a grid pattern east to west. And successfully uncovered two old soda cans, a beer bottle lid, and some sort of tent spike. None of them looked like they were part of the current site. Kirk had disappeared somewhere, possibly trying to trace a path from the campsite to the creek that would be plausible.

Zach turned his attention to the trees. And sighed deeply. This could take a while.

"I don't think this was an accident."

Zach jumped and spun toward the sound of Kirk's voice. He still couldn't see him, though he could hear him crashing through the brush. "Why's that?" He didn't think it was an accident either.

"No way the rain flooded this little plateau, right?'

"Right."

"The body was dumped down there." Kirk finally emerged from the forest, paused, and pointed behind him.

"Agreed."

"No drag marks, per se. It's rained too hard to expect that to remain. But I did find this." Kirk held up a large, clear plastic bag with a blood-soaked sleeping bag inside it.

Other than the blood, it looked practically new. Maybe the killer had shot John Doe inside the sleeping bag and used it to drag his body to the creek. The body had floated away, but maybe the sleeping bag was snagged on something and stayed.

"Good job, man."

"Thanks. Find anything?"

"Not really." Zach swung the detector toward the next tree. It pinged. "Aren't you just the good luck charm?" He leaned the metal detector against the base and pulled the tweezers from his pocket. He separated some ragged-edged bark. Bingo. A round hole the perfect size for a bullet. *Thank you, Lord!* If they were lucky, maybe they could get another DNA source from the bullet.

Chapter Thirteen

Annalise's phone woke her from a fitful night's rest. "Yes?" She heard the anxiousness in her voice, the hopeful expectancy. There still had been no word from a kidnapper for ransom. How Celine must be feeling! Had the poor woman slept at all? At least Annalise could claim a few hours.

"Officer Baker?"

"Speaking."

"I'm calling from the crime lab. We have some results for you on the weapon."

She'd completely forgotten about the gun. In light of the newest case, it paled in the list of priorities. "Can you email me the results, please?" She gave her address.

"Of course. Sending it now."

"Thanks."

She'd deal with the gun later. Captain Brooks would understand. Speaking of. She dialed his cell phone. "Any news?"

"Not so much as a peep."

The tone in his voice matched hers. Frustration. Fear. Disappointment. "Thank you, sir. I'm on my way to the station now." They had to find a way to *do* something. The dogs had indicated Cody was taken by car from the curb in front of his house. A dead end. No dog could follow that trail. Today's task had to be one that took them in a new direction. Her head hurt. Her heart too.

She opened a new text to Dave, but her fingers froze when she tried to compose it. What on earth could she say? Should she say? There weren't any words that would be fitting. She needed the ones that would make everything normal again, and they didn't exist.

He'd left early. She'd felt the bed shake and heard him in the bathroom, but in her exhaustion, she'd fallen back to sleep. Maybe she should've gotten up and hugged him. Kissed him. Told him how much she needed him and appreciated him coming the day prior.

She threw off the covers and deleted the message. She had to get to work. Words for Dave would come later. Hopefully.

Cody squeezed his eyes shut as beams of the first light he'd seen in days—had it been days?—shot through a doorway and sliced open his eyeballs. His hand throbbed. He squinted and looked at it. A deep cut lanced his palm. The events of the night before came flooding back. It wasn't a nightmare, and it hadn't been days. He didn't think, anyway. The sound of his window shattering had made him jump clean out of his bed. With his heart pounding, he'd grabbed a shoe. A shoe? Why hadn't he grabbed the lamp or the bat in his closet?

But it hadn't mattered. Before he even knew someone was for sure in his room, thick arms had wrapped around him and a hand had clamped his mouth. He'd kicked and squirmed, but, clearly, it didn't matter since he was here. Why were there no more memories of the attack?

Footsteps stomped closer. He cringed and blinked. Everything was blurry from being blinded by darkness for so long.

"Brought you food."

Something thunked on the cement beside him, sending the savory aroma of pepperonis and cheese into the air.

He didn't want to want the food, but his stomach growled. How long had it been since he'd eaten?

"Where am I?"

The man hovering nearby grunted.

"What do you want?"

Another grunt.

Cody opened the box and bit into the first room-temperature piece. It was one of the best things he'd ever tasted. "Look, if it's money you want, I can call my dad." Could the man tell he was bluffing?

Before he could take another bite, the man was in his face, piercing him with a cold glare. "You know what I want, boy."

A shiver ran through Cody. What was this guy talking about?

The man smirked and backed away a few inches. He pulled something from his pocket and tossed it at Cody's feet.

Cody picked up the credit card and read the name. Brian Moss. It must have fallen from his pocket, like he'd worried.

"That your dad?"

Cody nodded.

"He hiking recently in the Smokies?"

"What? No." At least Cody didn't think so. "Ain't seen him in a month." His insides chilled. The hike he and Braden had gone on. The gun. He felt the blood drain from his face.

"It was you. I can tell by the look on your face."

Cody shook his head.

The man grabbed his face, pinching his cheeks in his massive fingers. "You know good and well what I'm talking about. Where's the gun?"

"I—I got rid of it. Dumped in some kid's yard."

"Where?"

"Up on Dairy Pond Road."

"Good boy." He released Cody's cheeks. "Now, where's the money?"

What money? "I don't know. I really don't." Cody shrank against the wall.

"Right. Cause you've been so good at telling me the truth so far."

"I don't. I—I swear!"

"Seems you need some more time to think."

The man set a gallon of muddy water next to him and backed toward the door.

"No! Please…please don't leave me in here."

"Then tell me where my money is!"

Cody covered his ears against the man's echoing shout and his eyes against the darkness thrust back over the room.

"Get over to the Bank of America, Baker."

"Yes, sir." Annalise rose from the desk where she and Captain Brooks had been discussing a plan for the last half hour.

"I'll get down to the interstate and check the security camera at the banks there. Pray we caught a glimpse of this guy somewhere between here and there."

"I am, sir."

She walked the short distance to the bank under a cloud-dotted sky. How could the day be so beautiful when inside she was being shredded with worry?

The cool air inside the lobby dried the beads of sweat dotting her forehead. Was fall actually going to arrive at some point this year? "I need to speak with the manager, please."

"Yes, Officer."

A woman in an attractive business suit greeted her in the lobby a moment later. "How can I help you?"

"I need to see all security footage from the past twenty-four hours."

"Is this about that missing boy?"

"Yes, ma'am."

"Ain't that such a shame? We were all just devastated to hear about it on the news this morning. And in our town. Nothing happens here." She giggled but stopped when she realized Annalise wasn't laughing with her. "Come right this way. Anything a'tall to help that poor boy's momma bring him home safe."

She led Annalise into a monitor room and typed in a series of commands. The last day and a half sprang to life on the television.

"Our ATM camera doesn't really face the street, but you'll see here that our front entrance camera has a clear view. Use the arrows to fast forward or rewind, just like a remote."

"Thank you."

"Just give a holler if you need me. I'll be in my office."

Annalise held her breath and studied the gray and black feed carefully. There had to be something here. Anything that would help them find Cody.

What must he be going through? Annalise shuddered. She didn't want to let those images take life. It might make them more real than she could handle.

It didn't take her long to realize there was nothing on the video feed. Her hopes sank a bit lower. What next?

"I broke up with Jo." Zach didn't wait long after Annalise's hello to share the news.

"I'm sorry to hear that. And I didn't even get to meet her. Though as much as you talked about her, I feel like I did."

Zach switched the phone to his other shoulder and spread cheddar cheese on his onion bagel. "She was cute. Blonde like you. Loved that I was an officer."

"Yes, I remember that particular point." She chuckled. "So why did you break up again?"

"She wasn't the one."

"Right." She cleared her throat. "Listen, I gotta run. I'm headed over to check on Celine."

"Any progress?"

"None."

The sadness in her voice tugged at him. "I'm sorry. Anything I can do?"

"Pray."

"I have been. Hey, before you go. I found the bullet."

"Huh?"

"From the campsite."

"Oh, yeah. That's great. Congrats."

"Kirk says hi again. We know it's terrible timing, but we're both still crossing our fingers."

"I can't chat right now, Zach. I'll call you later."

She hung up, and he smiled. She hadn't said no this time. Or I don't know. She was getting closer to a yes any day now. As soon as he set his phone on the counter, it vibrated with another call.

"Special Agent Leebow?"

"Speaking."

"It's the lab. We have results for you."

Wow. This task force stuff sure had a way of speeding up normally sluggish-as-snail processes. "Okay, go ahead."

"The blood on the sleeping bag was a match to your John Doe."

"Great. How about the bullet?"

"No DNA on the bullet, but it matched a gun already on file."

Really? "That's great." Well, not great. If a gun was on file it meant it more than likely was involved in a crime already.

"Yes, an officer in a nearby town submitted it for testing. We lifted some fingerprints but nothing clear enough to make a match. Most of them were smudged, and we suspect someone tried to wipe it clean. We do know it had been fired recently."

Sounded about right. "Send me the full report, please."

"Yes, sir. On its way now."

He hung up and retrieved the email on his phone. No way. It really was a small world. Annalise's mystery gun matched his tree bullet.

Chapter Fourteen

Celine hadn't slept. The rings beneath her eyes screamed at Annalise as soon as the woman opened the door. A flash of hope zinged across Celine's eyes.

And Annalise's heart clenched. "I'm sorry, Ms. Moss. I don't have news."

"Oh."

"Have you heard from Mr. Moss?"

Celine shook her head.

Could Cody's father be involved? She made a note to order an APB on Brian's vehicle. They had given Celine enough time to try to reach him. "I need to talk to all of Cody's friends too. Can you give me names? Other than Braden. I know him already." That was her next stop, actually.

"Cody doesn't have friends. Not anymore."

Annalise didn't have the right words for this situation either. She was wrong. This was why she didn't want kids. This heartache. This fear. This terrible helplessness she felt for a mother she hardly knew and a child she'd found irritating but loveable.

She glanced at the kitchen clock. Closing in on thirty hours. She hated to leave Celine alone, again, but her work was outside this house's walls. "Do you have anyone that can come stay with you during this?"

A tear slid down Celine's face.

The officer waiting outside at the curb didn't provide much company or emotional support. "Could you call a neighbor? The townsfolk are so worried about Cody, and you."

Celine met her gaze. "They are?"

"Mmm-hmm. They want to help, but no one knows how."

"Several ladies have called from Norris Fellowship. Cody and I went twice for services there."

"Oh, good. Let someone come be with you. It doesn't make you weak or needy."

Tears splashed onto the countertop. Celine nodded and bit her lip. "Thanks."

"I'm going to speak with Braden. I'll be back to check on you soon, if I'm able."

Braden's house, situated on the other side of the half-moon commons, was a short walk. Annalise knocked on the door.

Braden answered, and his face paled.

"I need to speak with you."

He swallowed hard. "Okay. But I don't know nothing."

How was it that people who knew more than they were willing to tell always said the same thing? "Can I come in?"

Braden let the door swing wide and disappeared into the dark depths of the house.

Guess that was an invitation. Sort of. She stepped through, let her eyes adjust, and then shut the door. Following the sound of the television, she found Braden sitting in the living room. "Is your mother or father home?"

"Nope. At work."

"You're here alone?"

"Yep. I'm old enough."

She wasn't implying he wasn't. "Why aren't you at school?"

His gaze darted sideways and then back. "I'm sick."

Right. Maybe he was bummed out about his friend missing? "Listen, Braden, I'm going to level with you."

He muted the television.

So, she at least had his attention, if not his eye contact. "Cody's been missing for over twenty-four hours. Every minute that passes, the less likely we are to find him alive." She let that sink in. "If you know anything that may help us find him, now's the time to be upfront with me."

He sighed and dropped his head between his hands. "I don't know if it means anything or not."

"What is it?"

"We found a gun. Last weekend."

"The gun in the wagon?"

Braden nodded.

Her heart sped up. "I need to know every detail you remember." Her cell phone rang. Oh, not now. What terrible timing. She pulled it out and glanced at the caller ID, then silenced Zach's call. He would have to wait.

"Cody and I went on a hike up in the mountains. We were looking for the old troll bridge."

"Troll bridge?"

"Yeah, there's a hike up there, and if you find the troll bridge, they say it's haunted. We thought it would be cool to say we'd been there."

"You're only thirteen. How did you get to the hike?"

He laced his fingers.

"Braden." She imagined that's what her voice would sound like in a motherly tone.

"We went with this high school guy. Paul. He got his license last month."

She jotted the name on her notepad. "Does Paul have a last name?"

"Dunno."

Helpful. "Okay, so tell me about the hike. Where did you find the gun?"

"We hiked forever. Good thing Cody had the sense to bring a pack with water and snacks, or me and Paul woulda been in trouble." Braden swallowed. "You're going to find him, right?"

"I'm trying my best."

"We heard a really loud pop, and Paul said it was a gunshot, but me and Cody thought it was a big tree falling. We got distracted looking for the tree, 'cause if it made that big a noise, it musta been a huge one. And we stumbled into this camp that wasn't inside the markers for the campground."

The one she and Zach had hiked to? Her heart skipped. "Go on."

"Paul started rifling through the stuff. Cody and me told him to stop, but he wouldn't listen."

"What happened then?"

"Well, Paul found the gun lying over on a stump kinda near the tent. He picked it up and dared Cody to fire it."

"And did he?"

Braden nodded. "He couldn't look like a wimp."

Oh, Cody. Had it never occurred to these kids they might have stumbled onto a crime scene? "Is that all?"

"As soon's Cody fired the gun, we heard something crashing through the trees. And we all took off on a dead run. But Cody and me lost track of Paul. When we got back to the parking lot, his truck was gone."

"He left you behind?"

"Yeah, had to call my mom. She was pretty mad."

"I'd say so. What happened to the gun?"

"Cody put it in his backpack while we were walking down into town. Once we got to the store, we called my mom and hid. You know, just in case someone followed us from the campsite."

At least they had enough sense to do that. "When did Cody ditch the gun?"

"The next day. He said he didn't want to be caught with it, so he wiped it down and dropped it in that little wagon on the way home from school."

She should scold them for their ridiculous level of negligence, but the look on Braden's face tugged at her heart. "Anything else you can think of that may be helpful?"

"No, ma'am."

She handed him a business card with her cell phone number scrawled across the back. "Call me if you think of anything. It doesn't matter how small it may seem."

He nodded and met her gaze for the first time since she'd entered. "Find him. Okay? He's my best friend."

She couldn't speak over the lump in her throat, so she just nodded. *Lord, please help me find Cody.* She'd sent the same prayer up a hundred times already. Hopefully, He was listening. And already had a miracle in the making.

Chapter Fifteen

Annalise headed back for the police station, dialing Zach as she walked.

He answered on the first ring. "You aren't going to believe this."

"Well, hi to you too, Zach." Annalise rubbed her forehead to stave off the ache forming.

"Sorry, hi. I'm glad you called me back. I have huge news."

"What?"

"Your gun was the murder weapon for my John Doe."

The wind flew from her. She had a feeling, but knowing the full extent of what Cody had stolen was huge. "Wow. I have news too."

"Oh?"

"Cody is the one who brought that gun to Norris."

He whistled.

Their cases were inextricably tied, and Cody's chances of coming home alive had just dropped significantly. She told him everything she'd learned from Braden. "What do you think?"

"I think those boys did a really, really stupid thing."

"Agreed." But they were just kids. And immature, foolish decisions aside, all she cared about now was saving Cody. "You thinking what I'm thinking?"

"Yeah. The murderer wants the evidence back, and he's willing to go to any lengths to get it."

A knot formed in her stomach. "What will he do when he realizes the gun is already in an evidence locker in Nashville?"

"I don't know, Annalise. We need to pray really hard."

She already was, but what if God's plan wasn't to save Cody? What if He had another lesson planned for them all?

"I may have a lead on the whiskey runner I mentioned. Want to go with me to talk to him?"

"Absolutely." She still wasn't sure how, but the two had to be connected. If one of the gang's men was dead, the boss would have to know something.

"Meet me at Sugarlands Visitors Center in an hour and a half."

"Deal."

Annalise parked her truck and hopped into his. "Hey. Where're we headed?"

"Little old cabin in the middle of nowhere."

"Seems fitting for a whiskey runner."

He chuckled.

"What's this guy's story?"

"Ah, Jimmy Vern Buchanan. Released from prison about a year ago, where he served eighteen months for illegal manufacture and sale of moonshine. Though his mafia fell to the wayside a bit while he was incarcerated, rumor is he's back in business. No one can figure out where his still is though."

Zach followed the road between the mountains, weaving around curves and through shadows and sunshine until he found the gravel drive, and turned left. Two snarling dogs lunged at his tires as he pulled in front of the cabin and parked. "Great. Got any t-bones?"

"Oh, yeah, keep those in my pockets."

"You never know." Zach waggled his eyebrows.

She giggled. "What now?"

She turned her face toward the passenger window, where a Rottweiler had planted his massive paws.

"Make a run for it?"

"Sure. You first."

It was Zach's turn to chuckle. He honked the horn.

The front door creaked open, and a shirtless man in overalls stepped barefoot onto the long porch. He could've been the poster boy for Tennessee moonshiners.

If Zach expected the man to react, he would have been disappointed. The guy whistled and shouted something to the dogs.

They instantly retreated under the porch.

"Pretty good magic trick." He tossed a grin Annalise's way. "Ready?"

"Locked and loaded."

"Good. You're my backup."

They stepped from the truck simultaneously. Growls erupted from the shadows, but none of the dogs made a reappearance. "Jimmy Vern?"

"Yeah, who's asking?"

"I'm Special Agent Leebow, and this is Officer Baker. We were hoping you could help us with something."

Jimmy Vern spat a stream of tobacco juice over the porch rail, narrowly missing Annalise's shined black shoes.

She grimaced and took a step back.

Zach would have to let that one pass. For now. He needed this thug to stay calm. "I wanted to show you a photograph and see if you recognize this man?" He held an eight by ten photo up and watched Jimmy Vern's response carefully.

"Why should I tell you?"

Ah, there it was. Not a denial. Jimmy Vern knew the deceased. No doubt about it. "Should I remind you of the terms of your parole?"

Jimmy Vern sighed and sank his hands deep into the overall's pockets. "Buster Helms."

"Okay, great. And how do you know Buster?"

"Let's call him an acquaintance."

"Fine. When was the last time you saw him alive?"

Jimmy Vern cocked his head to the right. "I dunno. Maybe three weeks ago."

He was lying, but Zach would let that slip too.

Annalise had slipped slowly toward the corner of the cabin and studied something in the distance.

Zach cleared his throat. She was onto something. "Any questions, Officer Baker?"

"What's in the barn, Mr. Buchanan?"

"Nothing much. Old tractor. I bale hay now. Make an honest living."

Oh, yeah, right. Such an upstanding citizen.

"Keep my horses back there. You want to see 'em?"

Pride laced Jimmy Vern's words. But the concerned look on Annalise's face hadn't dimmed. What had she seen or heard?

She shook her head. "That's okay. Maybe next time."

"Don't go far, Jimmy Vern. We may have follow-up questions."

"Murdered?"

Zach nodded. He bit his tongue to keep from adding "by you." "We'll be in touch. You call us if you hear anything."

"Oh, of course, Officer. Wouldn't dream of doin' anything else but."

"Thanks." Zach snickered as he slid back into the driver's seat and turned to face Annalise. "Everything okay?"

"Yeah. Just thought I heard something."

"Maybe the horses in the barn."

"Yeah, maybe. Too bad we don't have enough for a warrant. That old barn would be the perfect place for a still."

"No kidding. If I remember right, that's where he hid it before."

"Come on, let's get back and see if Captain Brooks has any leads now."

Zach winced at the hopeful tone of her voice. He didn't want to be the one to remind her it was probably already too late for Cody to come home in anything other than a casket. The dogs broke out in an even louder ruckus as they headed down the driveway.

Someone was here. The dogs wouldn't be going nuts otherwise. If Cody had a window down in this wet, dirty hole of a cellar, he could get their attention. Now that the drugs the guy had given him had worn off and he could move again, he could flag the person down. Could get out of this terrible black. Could get home.

Where he would clean his room every day and get *A*s in math from now on. And hug his mother and respond when she said, "I love you."

He'd pounded on the wall when the dogs grew quiet a bit ago. A lot of good that did him, his aching hand reminded him. Though he couldn't see them, he imagined the walls were old river stone. Smooth, cold. Soundproof.

Earlier in the day, when the sun had positioned itself just so, Cody got one tiny little beam of light through a hole in the cellar door. He'd sat in that one pinpoint of light until it shifted away. If he'd been smarter, he would have stuck something through it. Something that would yell, "Hey, someone's trapped in here!" to any passersby. Like people stuck in trunks did by poking their finger out the taillights.

But now the dogs were barking again and sounding farther and farther away.

"Help!" His voice sounded so loud in his prison, but he knew it didn't make it through the floorboards. "Please! I'm here!" He pounded on the floor where he could reach it, near the door.

But the dogs grew quiet again. He hugged his injured hand close to his chest and sighed. He'd missed his chance.

Chapter Sixteen

Annalise pulled into Celine's driveway just before dinnertime. She answered her jingling cell phone. "Officer Baker."

"Hello, ma'am. We have lab results for you."

Annalise exhaled. She knew they'd rushed the results because of the nature of the case, but it felt like it had taken them weeks rather than a day. "Go ahead, please."

"All evidence at the scene matches the missing child."

No. That wasn't at all what she wanted to hear. "Okay, thank you." She dropped her head to the steering wheel. *Lord, I don't know what to do. Every lead we have turns out to be a dead end.*

She stepped out of the vehicle and cocked her head. What in the world? Raised voices echoed around the house, from the rear. She jogged through the side yard and stopped at the corner. A man, head and shoulders taller than Celine, stood over her while she sobbed. Where was the officer assigned to the Moss home?

"How could you let this happen?" he shouted.

Celine cowered.

"Sir, I'm going to have to ask you move away," Annalise said as she emerged from the bushes.

The man spun, opened his mouth to speak but apparently changed his mind, and took a few steps backward.

Celine turned round eyes Annalise's direction.

"What's going on here?"

"Officer Baker, this is Cody's father, Brian."

Oh. Finally. "I'm going to need to ask you some questions."

Brian spun and thrust a finger toward Celine. "She let our son get kidnapped, and you have questions for me?"

"What do you care?" Celine sprang around Annalise and returned the finger pointing.

"He's my son! Of course I care!"

"Hey, hey, hey. You two are going to have to cool it." She stepped in between them. "Celine go inside. Brian and I need to have a chat."

"Yes, ma'am."

Annalise waited until she heard the door click, then asked Brian to join her at the patio table. "I can't imagine how you must be feeling."

"No, you can't." He slumped into the seat she scooted back for him.

"We need to focus on what we can do, not what we can't."

He nodded. "Fine."

"We have been trying to reach you. Where have you been?"

"On a cruise. As soon as we landed this morning, I turned on my phone and got all these messages from you guys and Celine. I got the first flight from Miami home and came straight here."

That would explain his lack of communication, and it would provide him an airtight alibi. She made a note to verify his travel arrangements. "Can you think of any reason why someone would want to take Cody?"

He leaned back and crossed his arms over his chest. "No. We aren't rich people."

It was too soon to share her new theory with him. She needed to speak with Paul first. "Do you know who Cody has been spending time with lately, outside of school?"

He shook his head. "I, um, haven't been around much lately."

"Okay, well, we need you to remain close for now. Where are you staying?"

"Hadn't gotten that far. Cab dropped me at the curb and well, you know what happened next."

"Stay here." Annalise let herself in through the back door. "Ms. Moss?"

"In the living room."

Pictures of Cody when he was younger lined the hallway into the living room. They tugged at

Annalise. One, in particular, of him when he was probably five or six, holding up a fish with a huge grin on his face caught her. If only they'd known then what they knew now, they could have kept him safe. "I'm taking Brian to a hotel. Have you heard anything more?"

"No."

"Where is the officer that is supposed to be here?"

"I sent him home. They aren't going to call." Her voiced hitched. "Besides, you can monitor it remotely. I don't want the reminder staring at me every second. I lost my boy, and there's nothing anyone can do to make me feel safe anymore."

Somehow Annalise could relate. Though it wasn't her son missing, Annalise didn't feel safe anymore either. The carpet was being yanked out from under her in slow motion. "Braden told me about a boy named Paul. You know who that may be?"

Celine picked at a hangnail while she thought. "Paul Martin maybe? They played Little League together, but he was older."

Sounded like it could be right. "Thanks. I'll be in touch as soon as I hear anything." Thirty-eight hours and counting. Were the minutes zipping by more quickly the closer they got to forty-eight? It certainly seemed like it.

She dropped Brian at the Marriott and dialed Captain Brooks. "Any news, sir?"

"I've been knocking on doors and talking to potential witnesses all day. I've got nothing." He sighed. "TBI's been chasing down every lead they could think of too. Had an elderly woman tell us she saw a suspicious truck, and she even wrote down the plate numbers. Turned out to be one of those new delivery food drivers. It's like the boy evaporated."

Annalise sighed. That's exactly what it was like, but she certainly didn't want to accept it. "Have you heard of the Moonshine Mafia?"

"No. Why?"

Annalise updated him on everything that had happened with Zach. "It's the only potential lead I've got right now."

"Run with it."

"Oh, and I need an address for a high school kid, Paul Martin. You know him?"

"Yeah. Plays baseball with my son. Lives out on Highway 61. I'll text you the address."

"Thank you, sir."

Paul's house was a low-roofed, one-story with an overgrown lawn and five half-pieced-together vehicles dotting the landscape. She'd never paid particular attention to it, but now that she parked in its pot-holed driveway, she had some questions. Paul was only sixteen. Was he living alone? If he wasn't, why was the place so unruly? Flags shot up red warnings in multiple compartments of her mind.

Blue and red lights flickered at a seizure-inducing pace from one of the windows farthest from the front door. She knocked twice but, getting no response, made her way slowly to the window and glanced in. The strobe of colors made her head hurt, and she wasn't even in the room with it. "Paul? Paul Martin!"

The curtain jiggled, and a pale face flashed briefly through the window.

Oh, great. He was going to run. She could just feel it. Annalise bolted for the rear of the house in time to see a skinny, shirtless boy fly through the screen door and race down the rickety back steps.

"Stop! I just want to talk."

"That's what they all say!" he hollered over his shoulder as he made a break for the trees behind the house.

Innocent people didn't run from police officers. Unless they were scared kids. In the brief moments while she watched him flee, before he disappeared into the shadowed forest, Annalise had the sudden urge to scoop him into her arms and hug him. Had the poor boy ever had that kind of motherly affection?

She shook her head, and lifted her cell phone. "I'm going to need some backup." If he had the courage—or the terror—to run, he knew something she needed to know.

With her spotlight in hand, she slowly made her way closer to Paul's last location. "I swear, Paul, I'm not here to hurt you. I'm just trying to find Cody. I was hoping you could help me."

Silence.

"Braden said you all went hiking last weekend. I think you may have stumbled onto something that got Cody in trouble." She panned the light across the tree trunks again. Could he even hear her anymore? "I don't want anyone else to get hurt. Please come out."

Clearly this wasn't going to work. He could be halfway to the next county by the time her assistance arrived.

She pulled up information on the residence at her car's computer. Orrin Martin, age twenty-four, was listed on the deed. Far too young to be Paul's father. Brother, maybe? Something wasn't right here. If Paul lived with his brother, where were their parents? And why wasn't DCS involved?

Maybe they already were. She dialed the number for the local child protective services agent. "Cathy, Officer Baker here with Norris Police Department. I need some information on a family. The Martins at 1381 61 West, Norris."

"What now?"

"You're familiar with them then?"

"Orrin and Paul. Parents died six years ago. Orrin took custody of his little brother. Nothing but trouble since. What have they gotten themselves into now?"

"I'm not certain yet. Do you have contact information for Orrin?" Annalise wrote down the number Cathy provided. "Thanks. I'll be in touch."

"If you need my services, just give me a jingle."

Cathy sounded far too happy about that prospect. "I will. Thanks again." She dialed the number Cathy had given her, but it went to voicemail. "Orrin Martin, I need you to call me when you receive this message." She left her name and number. She didn't expect to hear from him.

Captain Brooks and a Clinton City officer pulled in from opposite directions just as she hung up the call.

"Hey, guys. Thanks for coming."

"What's going on, Baker?" Captain Brooks tugged his hat on.

"Paul ran."

"Great."

"Did you know DCS was involved in his custody and that he lives with his older brother?"

Captain Brooks shook his head. "Guess I shoulda paid better attention at the games. Well, let's find him."

Annalise pointed. "He disappeared there."

"Sure hope we don't have to get the dogs out."

"Me too."

The Clinton City officer nodded and stepped in behind the captain.

They fanned out, each with their own spotlight, and formed a line as they entered the trees. Good thing this section wasn't huge. And the rear border, if she remembered correctly, was a broad, swift creek. Hopefully, Paul had more sense than to try to ford it on foot.

"We just want to talk, Paul," she repeated. "You and Orrin aren't in trouble." Yet. Maybe the boy was really running out of fear and not guilt.

"Got something!"

Annalise turned in the direction of the Clinton City officer's voice. There was the sound of a scuffle and then a moan.

"Got him."

She broke into a jog and found Paul handcuffed, sitting at the officer's feet, and Captain Brooks hovering over them both. With his downcast face and his scrawny, pale torso, he looked as if he were twelve rather than sixteen. Her heart lurched. What had this boy faced in his short life?

Paul slowly raised his eyes and gazed at her. The purple and green bruise ringing his eye spoke volumes.

"Who did that to you, Paul?" she whispered.

He pressed his lips together.

"Listen," she knelt in front of him, "I promise I want to help you. And I want to help Cody too. I know you know him."

Paul's eyes darted away and then back to meet hers.

"If we take the cuffs off, can we trust you to walk back to the house with us?"

He shrugged his shoulders but then nodded.

She tipped her chin to the officer, and he released him. Captain Brooks and the officer flanked her. True to his word, Paul didn't fight them as they made their way back to the house.

"Guys, can you give us a minute alone?"

Captain Brooks and the Clinton officer nodded. "We'll be close," the captain added, pinning Paul with a fierce, protective look. "Don't do anything dumb."

Paul sank onto the top step, and Annalise took a position at the base. "You know Cody's missing, right?"

He nodded.

"I think you can help me."

"Don't know nothin'."

"Look, I already know about the hike. I understand you not wanting to tell me anything, but whatever you say goes no further than me. Got it?"

He nodded again.

"Can you tell me anything that might help at all?"

"Nope."

She mentally growled. Of course not. I get it, kid. You're stubborn and scared, but come on. She took a deep breath and blew it out slowly. "Cody took a gun from the campsite. Did you take anything?"

Paul's gaze darted away and back.

His tell was very telling. "What did you take?"

He glanced at the front door.

"Something inside?"

"No. Nothing. I swear."

"You're inspiring a lot of confidence, Paul." She didn't mean for the sarcasm to seep into her words, but he was trying her patience. "Can I come in?"

Fear flashed across his eyes. "Don't have to let you in, lady."

"No, I suppose you don't." She hated to threaten the kid, but what choice did she have? "But I can call Cathy, and I guarantee you do have to let her in."

His face paled. "Fine. Help yourself."

She slid past him. "Stay put." And let herself in through the front door. The stench of old cigarettes and burnt food greeted her. Not to her surprise, dirty laundry and ragged carpet sprawled the expanse of the small living room. When Paul ran, apparently he forgot to stop whatever video game he'd been playing. The hyped, loud music spilled down the hallway. The boys lived in squalor. How had Paul put up with it for so long? And how could DCS possibly think these were good living conditions?

The bedroom sported nothing but a bed, clothes baskets full of laundry, and sheets draped over the one window instead of curtains. A brand-new Nintendo Switch and several games sat on a crooked table in the corner.

She made her way back to the porch. "Did you take money from that campsite, Paul? Is that why you ran and left Cody and Braden behind?"

He dropped his head between his knees.

"Listen, I'm not mad. I don't know you from Adam, so your behavior can't disappoint me. But what I do feel is scared. The owner of the gun Cody took killed a man, with that very gun. And now

Cody's missing. Looks awful suspicious the two are related, don't you think?"

Paul didn't move.

"What if he comes looking for you next?"

"Can take care of myself."

"Clearly." There was that unintentional sarcasm again. "Where's your brother?"

"Dunno. Ain't seen him in two days. He took the car and took off."

They both knew what the next step would be. Whether she wanted to or not, she had to place that call to Cathy. Paul couldn't stay here in this nasty house, with a murderer on the loose and his "caregiver" missing. A foster home would have to be better, wouldn't it? She knew Paul wouldn't think so. She didn't have a choice.

"Did you spend all the money?"

Paul nodded. "Needed food, and paid the electric and water and house payment. Not that this dump is worth the money we pay."

This poor kid! Life had forced him into adulthood before he was ready. Before he could possibly be mature enough to handle it.

Lord, what do I do?

What if she stood in for a foster parent for a few days? Just until a good place could be found.

The thought took her breath. Was she really even considering it? She could keep Paul safe. And maybe the boy would open up more and remember something that would help her find Cody.

Annalise whipped out her phone and dialed before she lost her nerve. "Cathy, we need you."

"Figured as much. I'm already on my way."

Chapter Seventeen

How long would it take the cops to find him? Cody scooched into the corner farthest from the door. His stomach growled. He swigged the last of the grimy water and hoped it would at least make him feel full for a little while.

The man hadn't checked on him in a long time. Maybe it was time to start trying to dig out of this place with the little piece of two by four he'd found this morning. Was it just this morning? He would give anything for a flashlight and a watch. And some food.

And he could probably use some medicine for his hand. Every time he moved, he felt something wet seeping out of it. That probably wasn't a very good sign.

His eyes slid closed. There wasn't much else to do but try to sleep. Maybe he'd have another dream about home, and, for a few moments anyway, he could pretend he was safe and well fed and warm.

The cellar door flung open, the crash making him jump.

"What are we gonna do with him, Jimmy Vern?" A voice Cody hadn't heard yet filtered down the concrete stairs.

He was surprised to see that it was pitch black outside. When had nighttime fallen?

"That boy knows something. I ain't doing nothing with him until he tells me where my money is." Jimmy Vern stomped down the stairs and into view. "Had time enough to think, boy?"

"I swear, I don't know anything about any money."

"All right, say I believe you. Tell me what you do know."

"Nothing. Nothing, I swear." Cody didn't like the tremor in his voice.

Jimmy Vern bent close. "You're a liar."

Cody ran the memories of their hike through his mind. Nothing else had happened. He'd taken the gun. Ran. Went home and dumped the thing. And then Jimmy Vern had grabbed him. He shook his head.

Jimmy Vern slapped him.

A bolt of lightning ran through his jaw, into his head, and down his spine. Hot blood trickled down his cheek, and tears sprang to his eyes. No, he would not cry. He couldn't.

"Aw, look at that. Little fella cryin' for his mommy," the second man chided from the stairway.

"Who were you with, boy?"

Cody shook his head, earning him a second blow. His head bounced off the stone wall behind him. Black pulled in from the corner of his vision. "No one." He would not rat on his friends.

Jimmy Vern jumped to his feet. "Fine. No food until you talk. You hear me?"

Cody nodded.

"Glad you understand. I mean business. You will tell me where my money is, or you will die with your little secrets."

"Thanks, Kirk." Zachary hung up the phone and paced his living room. Kirk had touched base with TBI and gotten a firsthand update. Though they had nothing directly related to Cody's kidnapping, they may have something related to the Moonshine Mafia. In a roundabout way, maybe the one trail would lead to the other. After all, there was no doubt in Zach's mind Jimmy Vern was involved in both.

He put his phone on speaker, so he could pack. "Annalise?"

"Yeah?"

"What's wrong? Well, besides the obvious."

"Long story. I'll catch you up later. What's going on?"

"I'm headed to North Carolina. Over near Cataloochee."

"What? Why?"

"Well, not entirely sure yet. Some campers heard horses on a trail above the grounds, where there aren't supposed to be any horses."

"Okay, so someone broke a few trail rules. Why on earth is the SMIF getting involved?"

"The day before, the campers heard a loud bang and saw smoke."

"You buried the lead a bit there, didn't you, Zach?"

"Makes it more exciting that way. Something strange is going on, and Kirk and I are going to figure out what."

"Be safe."

"Want to tag along?"

"I kinda can't. I told you it's a long story. I want to hear what you find though, soon as you do."

"Talk to you in a few days."

He shot his mom a text, grabbed his bag, and headed for the truck. At a truck stop on I-40E, he parked his vehicle and hopped in Kirk's truck.

"Ready?"

Zach nodded, and though his thoughts should have been focused on the task ahead, he couldn't put Annalise out of his mind. She was worried about Cody, obviously. But something else was going on. Probably Dave. Maybe he really should call and give him a piece of his mind. He sighed. Nope. Still a terrible idea.

"You okay, man?" Kirk shot him a sideways glance.

"Yeah, just worried about Annalise."

"Kidnappings are always hard."

Zach nodded. "I don't think she's going to find the boy alive."

"Unfortunately, probably not. It's a sad but true fact of these cases that most victims don't make it home."

Zach knew Kirk must have seen some gruesome and unbelievable things during his time with TBI. Would Zach have to say the same thing someday? He'd been so excited about this opportunity, he'd never stopped to think about that aspect. There was a reason why task forces like these were called special. It certainly took a certain mentality to be able to work heinous crimes and not lose one's sanity. Maybe he shouldn't be pushing Annalise so hard toward joining him after all.

"This is the living room." Duh. Annalise wanted to roll her eyes at her own wit. "And the kitchen is here. The guest bath is down the hall."

Paul dutifully followed her without making a sound.

"And, here is your room." She spun to face him. "Look, I know this is weird, but…" But what? "Anyway, you'll find extra towels under the bathroom sink, and help yourself to anything you want in the kitchen."

He tossed his backpack on the bed. "Thanks."

"I'm going to go change. I'll check on you in a minute."

He didn't respond.

It was midnight. Where was Dave? The empty driveway practically screamed its loneliness when she pulled in. She dialed with shaking fingers.

He answered, sounding as if she'd awakened him. "Hey, hon."

"Hey." She smoothed the frustration in her voice. "Where are you?"

"Got a hotel up here in Gatlinburg. Didn't you get my message?"

Would she be freaking out so badly if she had? "No."

"I'm sorry. I tried to call, but you didn't answer."

"Oh. When was that?"

"Coupla hours ago."

She sucked in a breath. "Is everything okay?"

"Just wanted to get an early start in the morning. Thought I'd save the gas too."

By paying for an expensive hotel room? "Look, I have something I really need to talk to you about." She glanced at the closed door, imagining the scared, tough kid just down the hall.

"Okay…"

"We have a house guest for a few days."

His voice dropped several octaves. "Who?"

"You know the boy who was kidnapped?"

"You found him?"

Oh, how she wished she could say yes. "No. It's a friend of his. I'm kind of being his protective detail for a bit until we can figure everything out."

"Really?"

The tone in his voice wasn't what she expected. He sounded surprised but not angry. And suddenly she wanted to open up to him. To share all the thoughts and fears and feelings these boys had elicited for the past couple days. "You're not upset with me?"

"Nope. Surprised you are letting a kid stay with us but not upset."

She sighed. "Thanks, hon. Want to hear about him?"

He yawned. "Maybe in the morning."

Oh. She frowned. "Okay. Love you."

"You too. Good night."

By the time she changed and checked on Paul, he was sound asleep, looking vulnerable and small in the queen-sized bed. He may pretend to be tough when people were looking, but he was as terrified as any child should be in his situation, wasn't he?

Chapter Eighteen

Zach zipped open his tent and stepped into a foggy, gray morning. Warm for fall, down in the Cataloochee valley. Maybe they'd get lucky and see an elk or two today too.

Kirk already waited on a stump, gnawing on a protein bar. "Ready?"

That seemed to be Kirk's favorite greeting. "Let's go." Zach ate his peanut butter bar as they drove the short distance to the end of the road, and then he tucked the rest of the box into his backpack. Who knew how long of a day lay ahead of them?

TBI had given them the information for the trailhead's location, but past that it was an open board of possibilities. Endless, rolling mountains of possibilities.

"That seem odd to you?" Kirk directed Zach's attention to the truck and trailer tucked in a side road.

"Looks like someone tried to hide it, doesn't it?"

"Exactly what I was thinking."

"Why on earth would someone want to bring a horse trailer down that crazy, switch-backed, narrow, gonna-kill-you-if-you-take-the-turns-wrong road?"

"Good point."

"Either there's an incredible horse trail with an amazing, must-see view at the end, or these guys are crazy."

"Or up to something illegal." Kirk squeezed around the side of the trailer, between the close-sitting embankment. "No plates on the truck either."

"Even better." Why hadn't the park rangers noticed the vehicle and called it in already?

"They only work weekends here. With an occasional pass through the campground when visitors are present."

"You read my mind. So, these campers that reported the incident. Are they still here?"

"Left yesterday around lunchtime. Got their contact information though."

Zach nodded. "It's going to be a beast towing this outta here." He chuckled. "Or even getting a tow truck in here to start with."

"Another excellent point." Kirk rubbed his chin. "Let's say we hike up this road a ways instead of the trailhead."

It would've been easy to confuse the directions. From the campground, anything that happened down on this end of the valley would've seemed like it came from the trail. More than likely the people on the horses, with their unplated truck, didn't care so much about trails either.

"How do you suppose they got in here without anyone noticing?"

"Maybe someone did but didn't think anything about it."

"Or maybe they came in the lower road?"

"I don't think many people use that end. It's not very well maintained." Kirk smiled. "And perfect for someone trying to stay under the radar."

"It would've been a beast hauling a trailer and horses in on that road too. They must be pretty determined."

It wasn't hard to follow the trail the riders took, with the wet ground and patches of mud in the road. Piles of horse dung dotted their route. "How far does this old road go?"

"Top of the mountain. Used to be a fire tower. It burned down."

"Seriously?"

"Yep."

By lunchtime, they'd hiked as far as the side road would go, and the horse-track-trail continued, forging its own path through the dense forest. "Someone's done this more than once, wouldn't you say?"

"Mm-hmm."

"We should have brought the tents."

"Mm-hmm."

"You okay?" Zach turned to where Kirk sat with his head cocked to the side.

"You hear that?"

Annalise dropped her head to the table. She wanted to bang it against the wood. Maybe then she would have a breakthrough. Maybe then the clock on the wall wouldn't be ticking so loudly, driving thumbtacks into the worry center of her brain. Fifty-six hours and counting.

Fifty-six hours and counting.

Fifty-six hours and counting.

Annalist shot to her feet and paced down the hall to peek in on Paul again. She knew teenagers slept late, but it was after noon already. Should she wake him?

Millie followed at her heels, her claws clicking softly on the wood floor. She stuck her nose through the doorway and sniffed but sat at Annalise's feet.

Annalise bent to scratch her behind the ears. "Good dog," she whispered. Millie seemed to be watching over Paul too.

Poor kid was probably exhausted just from living his life. Her phone jingled, so she crept back to the kitchen before answering it. "Captain Brooks, please tell me you have news."

"Maybe something, but please don't get your hopes up too high."

Her hopes had bottomed out somewhere around four a.m., at the approximated forty-eight hour mark of Cody's abduction. She wasn't sure there was anywhere for them to go but up. At least a little. "What is it?"

"We had a call come into the hotline. A motorist passing through the area the morning of the kidnapping saw the news and thinks they may have seen Cody."

"Where?"

"At a gas station in Maryville. They had just left Cades Cove headed out early from camping, stopped to fuel up, and said they saw something suspicious."

"Oh?"

"The mom noticed a man open the back door of a dark grey Silverado. A child was in the backseat in an awkward position. She said it bugged her, but she brushed it off and thought maybe he was just sleeping."

"Okay."

"When they got home to Atlanta and watched the national news, they realized maybe the boy they saw matched Cody's description."

This was the first bit of information in two days that made sense. Eyewitness testimony was arguably unreliable, but what if just this once it panned out?

"I want you to meet a sketch artist at their home this afternoon, see if they can remember anything else while you're there."

"What about Paul?"

"Bring him on over. I'll put him to work washing the trucks."

"Oh, I'm sure he'll love that."

Captain Brooks chuckled. "Good for the boy."

"Right. Gonna have to wake him up first."

"He's still asleep? What kind of ship you runnin' over there, Officer?"

She giggled. "The kind that's never had a teenager before." Or any child for that matter.

"All right, get a move on."

"Captain Brooks?"

"Yeah?"

She chewed on her cheek and then sighed. "Do you think we're too late?"

The long pause was enough of an answer for her. When he finally did speak, his voice was clouded with emotion. "We will bring to justice whoever did this, God willing. It may be all we can do at this point."

She pressed down the lump in her throat. "Yes, sir. See you soon."

For a few minutes longer, she stood in the doorway and watched the deep rhythm of Paul's breathing. When she woke him, reality would come crashing back down into his world. And hers.

She touched his covered foot. "Paul? Time to get up."

He startled awake and looked at her with wide eyes.

Did he forget where he was for those first moments of wakefulness? "I have to go to Atlanta for work. Captain Brooks is going to hang out with you today. Okay?"

He nodded. "Give me ten minutes."

She let him get ready while she packed a cooler with some snacks and drinks for her trip. Pit stops were too time consuming.

Paul was silent on their drive down to the station, and Annalise certainly didn't know what to say. She had questions, but something held her from asking. "Want me to walk you in?"

"Nah." Paul swung open the passenger door and hopped out, slamming it behind him.

She waited until he disappeared into the firehouse to pull away. She'd known him less than a day and already wanted to make sure eyes were on him at all times. The man who'd taken Cody was possibly also a murderer. What lengths would he go to?

After swinging in to check on Celine briefly and then Brian, Annalise jumped on the interstate and aimed south.

Chapter Nineteen

A good fifteen minutes had passed, and whatever was stomping through the forest had yet to appear. Zach and Kirk stood on opposite sides of the end of the dirt road and squinted into the trees. How could something make so much noise and not be in their line of sight?

"See anything yet?"

"Nope," Kirk answered without looking away from the trees.

"It's got to be a deer eating acorns."

"Or an elk."

Finally, Zach spotted a sliver of brown between trunks.

A well-muscled buck stepped into full view.

"Kirk," he hissed.

"What?"

"Take a look at this fellar. He's gorgeous."

Kirk joined him and peered down a slight incline. "Wow. Trophy buck if I ever saw one."

They watched the buck work his way across the side of the hill, picking acorns from the downed leaves.

"He seemed awful calm, didn't he?" Kirk commented after the buck was fully gone from view.

"Yeah. Like he hasn't seen a human—or a horse—anywhere nearby."

"You read my mind."

"What now?"

"My gut is telling me to keep following the trail. You?"

"Yep. But we don't have enough supplies for a long haul through the woods."

"Think Annalise could help?"

"Maybe. What do you have in mind? I'll give her a call."

"By the time we hike back down to camp, she could be here with supplies. Then tomorrow morning, first thing, we hit it hard. By sundown tomorrow, maybe we can figure out where this thing goes."

Zach nodded even as he dialed Annalise.

"Hey, Zach. What's up?"

"We need backup."

"Now?"

"Sort of." He explained the plan. "Wanna help?"

"Yes, but I'm headed to Atlanta right now to meet a sketch artist. I can come to you as soon as I finish up. Probably around dinnertime tonight."

"That works. I'll text you a list of supplies we need. The SMIF fund will reimburse you later."

"If this helps find Cody, I don't care about being reimbursed."

He sighed. She was putting an awful lot of eggs in this one basket. "We don't know if this is related yet, you know."

"I am aware of that fact."

Ouch. He hated her snappy tone. It reminded him of when they were kids and she was about to rat him out to their parents. "Lise, you okay?"

"No." Her softened tone told him if he pressed any harder, she'd be crying.

"We're going to find him. And figure out what that snake Jimmy Vern is up to in the process."

"I hope so."

"If nothing else, getting you up here in the mountains will be a distraction while TBI, hopefully, works some magic and figures out where Cody is."

"The lady I'm going to meet thinks she saw him the morning he was kidnapped. Once I get her statement and the sketch artist finishes, we can get the image out on the news and maybe another concerned citizen will know something."

"Exactly."

"It's just…"

"What?"

"It feels like we're already too late. Like I've already failed him."

"Listen to me, Annalise. I know you take things to heart. That's part of what makes you so good at your job. But none of this is your fault. Whether we find Cody alive or not, it isn't your fault."

"Yes it is."

"Whoever took him, that's who we hold responsible. Period."

"You're right." She paused. "It's my first kidnapping, Zach."

"I know."

"I'm not sure I ever want to go through this again. Even in Memphis for those couple years, I didn't have one single kidnapping case."

"I know. It's got to be the hardest kind I can think of." He understood, but if she became part of SMIF, there was a good chance she would. His earlier thought returned. He had to stop encouraging her to take the job. He cared too much about her to see her suffer through another case like this. "Be safe getting here."

She sniffled. "I will. See you in a few hours."

"Thank you for agreeing to speak with me, Mrs. Marshall." Annalise stepped into a modest home in the outskirts of Atlanta. Two young children, a boy and a girl, peeked at her from behind the flaps of a play tent in the corner. She smiled.

"Oh, anything I can do to help."

The sketch artist extended his hand. "My name is Adam. I work with the police department. Do you have a table where I can set up my things?"

Mrs. Marshall led them into a small kitchen, with green gingham curtains and apple-dotted wallpaper.

"We don't want to take up any more of your time than is necessary," Annalise said as she sat at the table across from Adam and Mrs. Marshall. "But I was hoping you could go over, one more time, exactly what you saw."

"It was very early. Around five, I guess. We had to get home in time for my husband to go to work after a quick weekend trip up to Tennessee."

Annalise nodded.

"My kids were both sound asleep, but while Mark pumped gas, I happened to look over. And this pickup pulled in. A man got out. He glanced around, but I guess he didn't notice I was watching."

"Did you see any tattoos or birthmarks that may help identify him?"

"It was awfully dark, and foggy. I think he did have some tattoos, because he had a few gray spots, but I couldn't tell what they were."

"Do you remember on what part of his body they were located?"

Mrs. Marshall pointed to the base of her neck on the left side. "Here. And one on his forearm. I saw it when he got the pump handle out."

Just like Jimmy Vern. "Okay. Great."

"Well, anyway, he opened the back door and there was this boy laying there." She shook her head. "But he didn't have a pillow or anything. And his head was all cocked to one side. He looked very uncomfortable. I cannot imagine how someone could sleep in that position."

"Is there anything else?"

"I just had this feeling, you know. Something was off about the whole thing. The boy never moved. Not so much as a twitch." She wrung her hands on the table. "It was like he was drugged or something. I should've told someone then."

"We are glad you've come forward now." Annalise reached across the table and patted her hands. "Is there anything else you can remember?"

Mrs. Marshall shook her head. "I'm sorry."

"You've given us great information. Thank you. One last question, which gas station was it?"

"Pop's Gas 'n Go in Maryville. You know, right there on the main road?"

"Great. Thank you. I'll let you two get working then." Annalise rose from the table. "If you'll excuse me, I'm going to head on out. I have another lead I've got to follow. Adam, when you finish, if you could send the sketch straight to Captain Brooks, I'd appreciate it."

"Yes, ma'am."

"Thanks." She shook Mrs. Marshall's hand.

The kids giggled as Annalise walked by. She smiled at them again and let herself onto the porch.

"Captain Brooks, we need the video feed from the pumps at that little Gas 'n Go on the main strip."

"I'll get right on it."

"Thanks. How's Paul doing?"

"He's a great car washer."

Annalise chuckled. "At least feed him a good lunch for his volunteer time."

"Burgers at Little Senator do sound good."

"Anything new from TBI today?"

"Not a word."

"Zach and Kirk called earlier. They want me to bring supplies and hike back on a trail they've found. Is that okay with you? I can use personal time."

"No need for that. I'm getting the feeling whatever's happening up there in the mountains is related to our case too."

"I think they have to be. With the gun Cody stole, the murder of a man that's part of the Moonshine Mafia, and now this strange stuff up in the woods, I can't imagine it all being coincidence."

"Pigeon Forge and Cataloochee are directly across the mountain from each other. Sure wouldn't take much to get from one to the other by horseback, would it?"

"That's a good point, Captain."

"Keep me posted."

"You mind keeping an eye on Paul for a couple days?"

"It would be my pleasure. The ex-wife has the kids on vacation this week anyway. Paul and I can stay here, and the boys at the fire station can show him the ropes."

"Sounds like fun." It worked out well that their small town housed police and fire in the same building on occasions like these. School field trips were easy too.

Next she dialed Dave. Last night's restless sleep had been punctuated not only by fears for Cody but also inklings of a more sordid type about Dave's whereabouts. "Hey, hon."

"Hey. Any news yet on the boy?"

He'd remembered. Of course he had. It was all anyone in town could think about. "Maybe." She couldn't tell him the details though. That was something that always bothered her about her job. It made an impassable gap between them, like there was always something that kept her from being completely open with her husband. And she hated it. but she loved her job. "How's the job going?"

"Good. Should be home tonight."

"I'll be glad to see you."

He cleared his throat. "I gotta run."

A woman's voice sounded in the background.

Annalise couldn't tell what she said, but her heart thudded to life. "Who's that?"

"The client. She has a question. I will talk to you later."

"Love—" The line went silent. "You." Her sentiment floated over Mrs. Marshall's lawn, alone and empty.

She swiped sweaty palms down her thighs after tucking her phone into her belt clip. It was just a client. Just a woman Dave was fixing an air conditioner for. Innocent, harmless shop-talk. Her heart believed her, but her mind refused to relax.

Chapter Twenty

The smell of fried chicken reached Cody's nose before the sound of Jimmy Vern approaching did. Cody pulled himself against the wall and held his breath. His face and head pounded at the thought of another blow.

"Hey, boy. You hungry?"

What did this new, friendlier tone mean?

"I asked you a question. You want the food, you'll answer me."

Jimmy Vern's ugly, flashlight-lit face came into view.

Cody's eyes burned with the brightness. "Yes," Cody whispered. "I'm hungry."

"Good. Brought you KFC."

That meant Jimmy Vern had left. Cody's stomach dropped. He'd missed a chance at escaping. Not that he'd figured out how to get out of this stupid, wet, dark cellar.

"Eat up. Want some soda?" Jimmy Vern held out a large cup.

When Cody didn't make a move to take it, Jimmy Vern sat it beside Cody. Why was Jimmy Vern being so kind? A pang shot through Cody's stomach that wasn't just the hunger.

"Go on, boy. I ain't gonna bite." Jimmy Vern threw back his head and laughed.

Cody wasn't sure what was so funny. He tentatively picked up the red and white box and opened the top. His mouth instantly watered. No matter Jimmy Vern's motivations, food was food. He tore off a juicy chunk of crispy-breaded chicken and barely resisted the urge to moan, following it with a long, cold sip of Dr. Pepper. The juice and salt stung his hand as it ran down. Once the first taste melted in his mouth, all his resistance evaporated. He had never remembered feeling so hungry or eating a meal faster.

"There," Jimmy Vern leaned back in smug satisfaction, "Ain't that better?"

Cody nodded, just barely.

"I'm sorry 'bout yesterday. I lost my temper. I shouldn'ta struck you."

This was a trick. It had to be.

"All's I want is for you to tell me where the money is. Simple. Do that, and I let you go."

Maybe Cody should just tell Jimmy Vern about Paul. The jerk had left him and Braden behind after all. No. He was no snitch. He clamped his lips tighter together.

"Don't you want to get home to that sweet momma of yours?"

Cody did not like the light that danced in Jimmy Vern's eyes. Not one little bit. "Don't you talk about my mom."

"I'm sure she's real worried by now. Daddy too."

"Yeah, right."

"You've been all over the news, don't you know?" Jimmy Vern chuckled. "Well, how would you know? You've been stuck down here."

Again, Cody failed to find the humor. But he wasn't about to tell Jimmy Vern that little piece of information.

"Maybe I should just go pick her up too. I bet if I tossed her in here with you for a day or so, you'd both be about ready to talk. Eh?"

Chills ran down Cody's arms. The food he'd scarfed down threatened to make a reappearance. "I really don't know where your money is."

"But you know who does, don't you?"

He pictured his mom's face. Alone. Vulnerable. He had to do something. To point Jimmy Vern in another direction. "There was another boy with me." He'd tell about Paul, but he wouldn't throw Braden under the bus. Paul had Orrin to watch out for him.

"And? What was his name?"

"Paul. Paul Martin." Shame burned his throat. If only he had a way to warn Paul. To tell him trouble was headed his way.

"You think he took my money?"

"I never saw money. I swear."

Jimmy Vern smiled.

But it didn't bring Cody any comfort.

"I believe you. I really do. It's too bad you had to go and take my gun, Cody. Now the cops have it, and they are gonna pin something on me I didn't do."

Oh, yeah, like Cody believed Jimmy Vern was innocent. "I wiped it down real good before I dumped it. Didn't want my fingerprints on it."

"Good. That was real smart." Jimmy Vern sprang toward Cody and dropped to his haunches inches before him.

Cody recoiled.

"You'd better hope this Paul kid knows where my money is, or I may just decide to pay a visit to your momma after all."

When she agreed to meet up with Zach, she'd forgotten, momentarily, about Dave. That couldn't be a good sign. After seven years of marriage, her first thought should have automatically been to call and get his opinion. He wouldn't be happy about her being on an overnight trip with Zach. Her stomach filled with lead as she dialed. He would be upset that she had to cancel on him again.

When his voicemail picked up, she sighed. "Hey, hon. I'm sorry, but I won't be home tonight. I've got to run over to North Carolina and follow a lead on Cody's kidnapping." What was it people said? An omission of full truth, but not a lie. "I love you. I'll try to call you when I know more."

Her relief was short-lived. On its heels more doubts than ever. Something was wrong with Dave. Something was wrong, and in the pit of her heart she feared she already knew what it was.

She shook her head and drew her focus back onto the horrible, death-defying road before her. How on earth did people bring campers down this road? How did whoever brought that horse trailer in do it?

A text from Captain Brooks had come in just before she started the descent into the Cataloochee Valley. The APB had gone out on the truck and a description of the man, along with the sketch. *Lord, please let someone recognize them. Please give us something substantial to go on. Strengthen Brian and Celine while they wait. And, Lord, please, I beg you, keep Cody alive until we can get there.*

Zach and Kirk were the campground's only occupants.

She pulled into the parking space and waved. She checked her email but found she had no signal. Too bad. She wanted to see the sketch. It would probably have to wait until she got to the top of the mountain.

Zach's mouth stretched into a broad grin. "'Bout time you made it."

She stepped from the truck, and Zach immediately pulled her into one of his famous bear hugs. The tension she'd brought with her from Tennessee melted from her body and drifted away on the summer night's breeze.

"I'm glad you're here." He planted a kiss on top of her head.

"Yeah you are. I brought food."

"Precisely."

The three of them worked together to unload the gear she'd brought. They whipped up a quick dinner of roasted hot dogs and baked beans and sat around the dying fire munching Oreos. Tomorrow would be a beast, and who knew what would happen with either case. But for the moment, Annalise relaxed into the camp chair and shut the worry-wheel down for the night.

Zach couldn't sleep, though he knew he desperately needed to. The way Annalise had softened into his arms when she arrived brought back memories of their childhood. Since she'd married Dave, something about their connection had changed. Obviously. But he missed her trusting him completely with every problem she had. Missed being the one to make it better, or if he couldn't fix it, at least make her smile.

His best friend was hurting, and she was only a few feet away. The only thing between them a few sheets of canvas and Kirk. When this case was over, whether Annalise joined the task force or not, he would be a better friend. Would be more available for her. Something told him she was going to need that more than ever before.

Four a.m. came before he was ready for it. But the alarms on Annalise's and Kirk's phones sounded, and he knew the time for fighting to get sleep was over. In a way it was a relief. He should sleep like a rock tonight.

They each packed their tents and added them to their packs. Kirk took the lead, and Zach hung back with Annalise. "What's Dave think about all this?"

"Don't know. Haven't talked to him."

"Think he'll be mad?"

"I'd like to say no, but I have a feeling he will be."

"When did he start hating me so much?"

"I don't know."

"Ouch. I thought you would at least say, 'He doesn't hate you, Zach.'"

"I'm sorry. I can't say that, because I honestly just don't know what's going on with him."

"Do you think—" he shook his head. "You know what, never mind."

"It's crossed my mind, I'm not gonna lie."

How could Dave even think about leaving someone like Annalise?

"So, what do you know about this whole thing?"

"We know the truck doesn't have plates and the horses went in a direction where there are no marked trails, by foot or horse."

"Have you looked at the map?"

He zipped his pack. "Not really. I mean, I know in my head where we're at."

"Directly, almost a straight line, across from Pigeon Forge."

"That right?"

"I don't know what to expect, but my gut is telling me Jimmy Vern found a new location for his moonshine operation."

Chapter Twenty-One

What did the dried corn mean? The little individual kernels had dotted the path for about half an hour. Had the guys noticed them? Food for the horses, maybe.

Or fodder for the whiskey.

"Zach?"

"Yeah?" He stopped right in front of her and took a swig of water.

"Look down."

A yellow kernel lay next to his right boot. "What do you make of that, Annalise?"

"Corn whiskey?"

"Think this is the supply route for the still?"

"I'd say it's a good bet."

Kirk had finally noticed their lag and returned. "What's up?"

Annalise pointed to the ground.

"Oh, yeah. Good eye."

She held her head high. "Thanks."

"There was corn in the tent where Buster was shot too," Zach added.

"Yeah, there was." Kirk took a swig of water.

"We probably ought to start looking for a place to camp, don't you think, guys?"

They nodded and resumed hiking. Annalise kept her eyes peeled for a suitable site, and she knew the guys were doing the same thing.

It was her favorite time of day. When the sunbeams hit the world at acute angles, lighting the leaves like paper lanterns. Whoever had ridden through forged their own trail, but they'd done it frequently enough that hiking in their tracks was simple. How had the park rangers in Cataloochee not noticed them? She stopped cold. Because they didn't always start in the park. Maybe they alternated entry points, all converging onto this one trail. She should have paid better attention to side-tracks.

"Zach?"

He stopped again, and this time she thudded into his back. "You're sweaty."

He chuckled. "Yeah. And your point is?"

"These guys are really well organized for a bunch of moonshine runners, don't you think?"

"It seems that way."

Her feet grew heavier with each forward step. What were they walking into? There was big money in moonshine. Someone seemed to be taking his business very seriously. Was it Jimmy Vern? Or someone following in his footsteps? If it was Jimmy Vern, he'd obviously learned some things from his first go-around with the law and adjusted his operation accordingly.

"We will have a dry, dark camp tonight. Okay, guys?" Kirk said from the front.

"Agreed," Zach said.

She nodded. No sense in tipping them off if they were up ahead somewhere.

Kirk stopped them in a depression, safely tucked inside rolling bumps on the side of the mountain.

"How old you think these trees are, Lise?"

"As old as the earth." She liked the thought of bedding down under the boughs of trees that had seen Native Americans gliding in the shadows. Deer that had never seen a man. Wild horses, native elk, and maybe even American Bison at some point. If they could share their stories, what would they reveal about the ages long past?

As quietly as possible, they set up camp and ate a light dinner of tuna and crackers. With her back to a rock, seated facing Kirk and Zach, Annalise watched the patches of sky turn black between the treetops. What was Dave doing right about now? Was he mad at her? Did he even care anymore?

She had to do something more than just hope and pray that things would be okay. When they got back, she'd find a Christian marriage counselor and see if she could talk him into going. He wasn't big on talking to strangers about his problems, but she would be able to convince him on this issue. It was too important not to enlist some extra support.

Was Paul okay? She chided herself mentally. Of course he was. Captain Brooks would protect him with his life, should it be necessary.

How about Cody? She'd pushed thoughts of him aside with the physical exertion. But it was taking her too long to find him. By dawn it would be seventy-two hours since his abduction. What had the poor boy endured in those three days? Had he even survived the first one? She shuddered. He may have been better off not making it through the initial twenty-four. Who knew what his kidnapper was capable of? There wasn't exactly such a thing as a normal, nice kidnapper.

"You okay?"

Zach's question made her jump. "Yeah."

"Thinking about Cody or Dave?"

Kirk's eyebrows lifted, but he didn't say a word. "Both."

No one seemed to know what to say. She didn't either. So they sat silently, listening to a barred owl calling to its lost mate. A profound sense of emptiness filled her from the bottom of her stomach, climbing higher until she felt hollow.

As darkness enveloped them, Zach clicked on his battery-operated lantern. He looked at her and then clicked it back off.

A moment later, she felt his strong arm around her shoulder. There was a rustling to her left, and Kirk's dark form slipped into his tent. She leaned into Zach's shoulder as hot tears streaked down her cheeks. She needed the release her tears brought. Holding in her fears and suspicions and worries was exhausting. *Thank you, Lord, for a good friend like Zach.*

Suddenly self-conscious, she straightened, shook his arm away, and swiped at her cheeks. "This is silly."

"Annalise…"

"I'm fine. I'll be fine. Come on, we should get some sleep." She tucked into her tent and zipped the door flap. As she lay down, the burdens she felt, both for her marriage and Cody, burrowed into a corner of her heart and took up residence. A dark, painful place she wanted to ignore but couldn't.

Would tomorrow bring resolution to any of her concerns? Or just more sorrow?

Morning sunbeams pierced the canopy of her one-person tent, bringing with them a glow, as if she was sitting inside the paper lanterns she'd imagined the day before. She wished she was. Or maybe a little fairy inside a sunlit tulip, not a care in the world, flitting from bud to bud. Singing a happy song that would lift her heart and make her forget reality.

As soon as she unzipped the tent and began packing, though, her fanciful notions vanished. She'd needed to let some of the stress out last night, but today was a new day. She was tough. Strong. Resilient. Everything would be okay, one way or another. She snorted. Especially if she kept ignoring all the negative emotions and pretending she was fine.

"All right, let's talk about the game plan." Kirk motioned for them to gather near him.

Annalise couldn't quite get a full, deep breath. What would they find ahead? Would they be outnumbered? Would there really be anything to find? And most importantly, could something out here, in the middle of nowhere, actually lead them to a living, breathing Cody?

"If we find a camp today, we will try to take them peaceably, obviously. However, I want you both to prepare yourselves for the worst. Should we run across a group that outnumbers us, we will hang back and wait for backup." He patted his shirt pocket. "I have the park rangers on standby with four-wheelers, but it will take a couple hours for them to get here. And there is no doubt the noise will alert them to our approach."

Zach nodded.

"And what if there isn't anything there at all?" Annalise voiced her most pressing concern. It actually scared her more to find nothing than it did to face shooting, violent men. Because if they found nothing, she was back to square one again.

"Then we hike with our hearts in our throats all day for nothing, I suppose."

Ugh. That idea sat well.

They silenced their phones and silently started up the trail. She kept her eyes more open for places where other branches could flow into this one and her ears strained for any unusual sounds.

It didn't take all day. Two hours into their hike, Kirk held up his hand. They all paused. Men's voices drifted through the trees, and the smell of a campfire greeted her nostrils. It could just be hikers, she supposed, but if it was, they were way off-trail.

They fanned out, with Zach on her left and Kirk on her right, and crept closer. She approached the next rise by slipping quietly from tree to tree. Without even needing to look, she knew the men did the same.

The voices grew louder.

She paused and made eye contact with Zach, then drew her weapon. He did the same. She had lost sight of Kirk somewhere, but he was there. Lurking, creeping, circling around to help.

A few hundred feet more, and she had eyes on the camp. Hidden under the canopy of dense trees and surrounded by thick undergrowth, three men worked around a large, copper still. Drawing water from a natural spring, one man fed the cooling apparatus while the other two appeared busy mashing corn in a stone basin, with the aid of one of the horses turning an old-fashioned grinder.

Wow. She had to give these guys some props here. They knew what they were doing and, clearly, had put serious time and effort into bringing the appropriate equipment this far into the mountains.

Kirk's voice rang out across from her and Zach. "Everyone freeze."

The three men jumped and spun to locate the voice, but it was too late. Kirk had stepped into their camp with his handgun aimed at the closest one. His hands shot up, dropping the metal pot full of water.

Zach and Annalise stepped out simultaneously. They'd always been able to connect on a subconscious level, to coordinate their actions without a word passing between them. The sound of their footsteps crunched on the fallen leaves, and the remaining two men turned their direction.

One drew a pistol from his waistband.

"Zach, look out!"

"I see him."

His voice was as cool as ever. How did he manage to keep his calm, when her heart was racing and throat was dry?

"But, you see, he ain't going to shoot me." Zach grinned at her, keeping his gun trained on the man. "He's out of bullets."

She covered the third man while Zach drew closer and removed the gun from the other man's hand.

The man cocked his head sideways. "How'd you know?"

"It's a revolver, bud. I can see the empty holes."

Okay, props-giving time over. These men clearly were not the brains of the operation.

Chapter Twenty-Two

Zach took a deep breath while Annalise had her back turned. That was close. He wouldn't tell her he was bluffing and that he couldn't be a hundred percent sure all the chambers in the gun were empty. She'd kill him.

The three arrested men sat on a log, their hands cuffed behind their backs. Kirk stood watch over them. The distant hum of ATVs buzzed the otherwise quiet summer air. According to the last radio transmission from the rangers on four-wheelers, it would take another hour for their ride out to arrive. The sound bounced off trees and up the valleys, growing louder as time passed.

"You okay?" He nudged Annalise's shoulder.

She nodded. "Glad we got them."

"But you're disappointed."

She shrugged.

"I get that. I was hoping Jimmy Vern would be here too."

"Yeah, well, maybe we can find something here that will tie him in and give us enough reason to go back to his place." She bit her cheek. "I can't shake the feeling we missed something. What if Cody was there all along? What if we missed our chance to save him? What if—"

"Annalise, stop. Don't go down the what-if road. You've done everything you can, within the limit of the law, to find the boy."

"You say that like you think it's too late already."

He did, but he wasn't about to confess that either. Maybe there was a miracle in the works, and somehow, Cody was still alive. But Zach was skeptical, to say the least. "Now, I didn't say that."

"I can tell by the look on your face, best friend. I've known you too long."

Zach hated seeing the hurt welling up in her brown-streaked hazel eyes. "That means you know I won't lie to you, if I can help it."

She started to turn, but he grabbed her by the elbow.

"And that I won't hurt you either. Not just if I can help it, but no matter what."

She nodded. "I know."

"Good. I hope you're the one who is right. I honestly do."

"Thanks."

He and Annalise combed through the site, carefully examining each detail of the men's belongings and the still.

"Check this out." Annalise emerged from one of the tents and handed him a couple of Sawyer water filters.

"Same as Buster's."

"Lots of people buy these though."

"True." He smiled. "But there's this." He handed her the small slip of paper he had found in the other tent.

"A receipt. Brilliant."

"Looks like they paid cash, but maybe we'll get lucky and find them on security footage." He pointed over his shoulder. "Found out what made the loud noise the campers heard. Come look."

She followed him into the edge of the woods. Lying discarded in the undergrowth, a large boiling chamber pot with its sides burst open sat on its side. Jagged metal stuck out at odd angles.

"Guess they had an accident."

"And needed a new one packed in on the horses." Annalise smiled.

"Makes perfect sense."

Annalise scrunched her brow. "Zach?"

"What?"

"Where're the other horses?"

Good point. Why hadn't he or Kirk noticed that yet? Zach squatted in front of the men. "Horses? Where are they stashed?"

The men squirmed but remained silent.

"Fine. Don't talk to me." Zach grinned. "We'll let Kirk chat with you when we get to headquarters."

Kirk glared at them and crossed his arms over his chest.

Zach chuckled as the men shrank subtly. Kirk had quite a reputation for his interrogatory skills. He could get information out of an inanimate object. A dead man to talk. And he never had to touch his victims. Zach still didn't know how, because no one Zach knew had ever seen Kirk's interrogations in person. Someone had at the TBI, Zach was sure of it, but they didn't talk about it afterward.

Hopefully, Kirk's reputation wasn't all smoke and mirrors. They needed these men to give them more. Annalise's ability to find Cody depended on it.

Another day's worth of his pitiful little sunbeam had come and gone. And he was still here. He hadn't seen Jimmy Vern since the fried chicken.

Cody's mouth had thanked him for the food, but his stomach had revolted. Curled up on the cold dirt floor, he didn't even want to think about the corner he'd been using as a bathroom or about what had happened there for the last day. He lifted his hand to brush a spider from his forehead, and shook with the exertion.

Why couldn't he just be a man and get up and break out of this place? The thought of what Jimmy Vern might do should he catch him in his escape made him tremble even more. He struggled to sit up and found his head throbbed with each breath, so he lay back down.

How many days had he been in this hole?

It didn't matter really. His mom, and now his dad for sure, were on their way. The police were waiting to rescue him until it was safe. And until they could nab Jimmy Vern at the same time. He just had to be patient. And strong. And keep fighting.

Right?

Annalise paced the forest edge surrounding the camp. How could these guys have hidden the other horses? It's not like they were silent, tiny hamsters. Each of the men had to have ridden one in to account for the separate sets of prints they'd seen. Based on the prints, one of the horses was considerably larger than the others, possibly a mule. Perfect for carrying the corn that had once occupied all the empty feed sacks.

Jimmy Vern had horses. Was it possible he had been with these men, dropped them off here with instructions, and then taken his mounts home with him?

She spun and stalked to where the men waited to be loaded onto the rear seat of the ATVs. "I know you had at least two more horses. Are they Jimmy Vern's?"

Still the men refused to answer.

She needed something to entice them. A reduced sentence or a get-out-of-jail-completely-free card. She would be willing if it meant finding Cody, but it wasn't up to her. After Zach and Kirk took these men in, she would have to go home and wait. Maybe she should just tell Kirk right here and now that she wanted the job. She stomped back to the tree line and resumed her pacing, chewing on her thumb as she thought.

What would get these stubborn goons talking? A hot iron? The fire under the still smoldered. She could—

No. What in the world could make her, even for a second, consider something like that?

"Annalise?" Zach waved to her.

"Huh?"

"Ready?"

They'd put each of the arrested men on a side-by-side ATV with two officers. Kirk waited on a four-wheeler with a park ranger at the steering and another on the back rack, and an empty ATV waited for her and Zach. She climbed on behind him, strapped on the helmet, and wrapped her arms around his waist.

She found comfort in the way his muscles moved as he steered down the mountain ahead of the side-by-side carrying the arrested men. In the way his breath flowed in and out and his heartbeat reverberated under her grip. But she wished it was Dave. How long had it been since they'd done something fun together? Just the two of them, relaxing and her not worrying about work or leaving in the middle of the night to go help someone she didn't even know.

That was why Dave had put distance between them, wasn't it?

Maybe when she got home, she'd ask him out on a date. Romance him a little. A candlelit dinner and a night in their backyard oasis staring up at the stars.

Who was she kidding? She couldn't take a night off and relax with her husband. Not while Cody was still missing and Paul was under her protective watch. But as soon as the case was over, she'd plan on wooing her handsome husband. They could fix things. She just knew it. She would prove to Dave how much she loved him and wanted him to be front and center in her priorities. As soon as she found Cody. And put his kidnapper behind bars for a very, very long time.

Chapter Twenty-Three

"I'm hungry," Zach said as he climbed into the passenger seat of Annalise's truck.

"You're always hungry."

"I feel like we've had this conversation before." He grinned.

"We have. Multiple times."

She slid into the driver's seat and started the vehicle, checking her rearview to make sure the officers lined up behind her. The arrested—and still completely silent—men accompanied by two officers each waited for her lead. Kirk brought up the rear. They planned to caravan back to Knoxville. Kirk and Zach would begin interrogations first thing tomorrow morning, after keeping them each in isolation the rest of the night. Kirk's interrogation techniques and preferences were different than other officers', but his track record proved he knew what he was doing.

"I'm tired."

"Geez, Zach. Is there anything not wrong with you right now?" She swallowed the bitter taste of her snarky words. "Sorry."

"Dave call yet?"

How did he know exactly how to find the painful knot hiding underneath and dig it out like a rotten potato turned free from its soil? "No—"

Her phone rang with Dave's special jingle. "Speak of the...never mind."

Zach raised his eyebrow.

Annalise rolled her eyes and answered. "Hey, hon."

"When are you going to be home?"

"Coupla hours. Everything okay?"

"No. Someone broke in last night."

"Are you okay?"

"I wasn't home."

Her blood turned cold. "Where were you?" He should've been home from Gatlinburg yesterday, way before bedtime. "Dave, you still there?"

"Yeah. The place is a mess. Millie's okay though. I had let her into the back yard for the day. I knew you'd be worried about her."

He hadn't answered her question. Was it on-purpose or distraction? She swallowed hard. "I'll be there as soon as I can. In the meantime, I'll have Captain Brooks come by and start the report." And what did he mean by worried about her? Like he thought she'd only be worried about their pet.

"I can't believe this. Is it tied to one of your cases this time too?"

A weight settled on her shoulders. An old one she recognized well by this time. "I…I don't know. Possibly."

"That's just great, Annalise." He huffed. "I don't know how much more of this I can take."

"I'm sorry, Dave. I really am."

"Whatever."

"We'll talk when I get there, okay? I promise."

"Righto."

She hated when he said that. On the surface, righto sounded like a plan, an agreement, a positive. Underneath, she'd come to learn, it really meant something far less enthusiastic. Something along the lines of "I don't want to talk about it because I'm so mad I may never forgive you. And I wouldn't believe your apology, no matter what you say."

She dropped the phone into the console cup holder and sighed.

"What's up?"

"Break in at my house. Dave's pretty mad."

"What are you thinking?"

"That work is affecting private life again."

"It happens sometimes in this business."

She slapped her palm against the steering wheel. "It isn't supposed to."

"Look, what happened five years ago was not your fault."

"Sure feels like it."

"What were you supposed to do?"

Keep her mouth shut and her head down.

"You couldn't have unseen what you saw. You did the right thing arresting that senator."

"Yeah, worked really well for me and Dave."

Zach put a warm hand on her shoulder and squeezed. "He broke the law, Annalise. Just because he had a position of power shouldn't mean he is immune. You saw him, firsthand, selling illegal prescription drugs."

"He wasn't just selling. He was running the ring."

"Exactly. You had to arrest him."

"His thugs didn't have to burn down my house." If she closed her eyes, she could still smell the smoke. Could still see the flames leaping from the windows as she and Dave watched helplessly from the curb. Their early years of marriage burning to mere ashes. Their first home, their photographs, their first pet never making it out alive.

And now, their home finally felt like a home again, and she wanted to ask Dave to move. What kinds of criminal masterminds would she encounter if she did work for the Smoky Mountain Investigative Force? Probably more than just a few drug dealers.

She chuckled. She hadn't even taken the job yet, and she was already dealing with one. Or at least suspected she was. The break-in seemed far too coincidental to not be related to Jimmy Vern and Cody.

At the top of the mountain, where she had full bars of service, she dialed Captain Brooks. "I need you to go to my house."

"What? Why?"

"Dave just called. There's been a break-in."

"I'll head right over. I can teach Paul about crime scene investigation."

"Is he doing okay?"

"Yeah. He's perked up a lot the last day or so. Even got five words out of him yesterday evening."

Annalise giggled. At least that was something going right. She hung up.

"You okay?"

"No."

"Did Dave mention me this time?"

Annalise shook her head.

"That's a good sign, right? Maybe Dave's coming back to his senses. He's crazy to think anything would ever happen between us."

"Oh, gee. Thanks. I'm so flattered."

Zach's face turned red. "You know that's not what I meant."

She slapped his shoulder. "I'm messing with you."

He blew out a breath. "Good."

"You're like my brother."

"Exactly."

She couldn't wait to get to the house and see the situation with her own eyes. If someone broke in looking for something or to steal things, that was totally different than if they simply trashed the place. If it was a robbery, it might not be related to Cody's case.

"You know," Zach paused and picked at a hangnail, "sometimes people make other people feel guilty to defer suspicion from themselves."

"Yeah." She'd already thought that ugly little thought about Dave too many times.

Chapter Twenty-Four

By the time she got home, the house was dark, save for one living room light. She stepped through the front door, holding her breath and expecting the worst. She wasn't wrong. Pieces of glass from the front window littered the floor. Magazines from the coffee table were strewn among the shards. The overturned chair held a gash down its entire back surface. The DVD tower had been slammed into the wall and lay in splinters before a huge hole in the drywall.

This was no robbery.

It was a message.

She wandered into the dark kitchen and set her bag on the counter.

"You're home late."

Annalise clutched her chest and spun at the sound of Dave's voice. "Hon, you scared me to death. What are you doing sitting in the dark?"

"We need to talk."

Something about his voice sounded odd. "I agree." About so many things. She closed her eyes and tried to still the racing of her heart. "I...I..." She didn't know exactly where to start.

He coughed and something clinked against the table.

She flipped on the light over the sink and turned slowly to face him. His watery eyes and slacked lower lip yelled at her that something was seriously amiss. "Are you drunk?"

"Only way I could have the courage to say what I need to say."

"When did you start drinking again?" It had been years since she'd seen him consume alcohol. He knew how much it bothered her. Her throat tightened painfully. "I can't believe this, Dave. You promised."

"You know what I can't believe, Annalise?"

She opened her mouth, but he didn't wait for her response.

"How your job has come between us again. You remember when we moved here? Your promise to me was that you wouldn't get so caught up in work that our marriage took a back seat ever again."

"I—"

He slammed his knobbly glass on the table. "Don't. Just don't. I know what you're going to say. That you didn't mean to. That you never mean to make me feel second fiddle. That you and Zach are still just friends. And that your heart belongs to me."

It was exactly what she was going to say, minus the Zach part. Her last position had come between them. She could admit that. She sank into the chair opposite him. Words failed her.

"I need a wife who lets me lead from time to time, you know?"

"I don't let you lead?"

"You're too independent. Too headstrong. Too self-sufficient."

She had never thought of those qualities as detriments. "Dave, I—"

He stared into his glass of clear liquid. "You don't need me."

"Dave, look at me."

He raised his gaze slowly to meet hers.

"You're right. I don't need you. But I want you. And I always thought that would mean more, you know. I can handle life on my own, but I choose not to."

He raised an eyebrow.

"I love you, and I don't want to lose you. Not for my job. Not to alcohol. Not to anything."

"I don't think I can do it anymore."

Searing pain sliced her heart. "Don't say that. Please. I was coming home and planning on telling you I think we should try marriage counseling with a Christian therapist."

"You were?"

"I know I'm not perfect. But no one is. We can be perfectly imperfect together."

"I don't know."

She reached across the table and squeezed his hand. "Don't give up on me. On us."

He yanked his hand free and took another swallow, grimacing as it went down. "It's too late. There's…someone else."

The breath flew from her lungs. She sat back into the chair. What could she say to that? "Gatlinburg?"

He nodded.

"Have you...?" she couldn't finish the sentence.

The seconds that passed felt like hours.

Ever so slowly, Dave nodded.

And, like the glass littering the living room carpet, her world shattered.

Zach stopped on Annalise's front porch and pulled his phone out, double checking the message.

"I need you."

Not too many ways to interpret that, other than to do exactly as he had done and show up. At one a.m. After trying to call five times and getting no answer. If he walked in the front door and met Dave instead, what would happen?

It didn't matter. His best friend needed him. He would walk through fire for her. He knocked but received no response. "Annalise?" he asked as he swung open the unlocked front door. Why on earth would she leave it open after a break-in the same day? She knew better.

Using his phone as a flashlight, he swung it round the room and stopped cold. She hadn't cleaned up? His pulse sped. "Annalise?"

A moan met him from the direction of her bedroom.

Had someone broken in again already and attacked her? He drew his weapon and pressed his back to the hall wall, slowly proceeding toward her room. If she was hurt…He didn't know what he would do.

He stopped at the corner and peeked in. A solitary lamp on the nightstand dimly lit the room. Annalise's blond hair coated her pillow, but he couldn't see her face. "Annalise?"

She dug a hand out from under the covers and waved.

"Are you okay?"

"No."

"Who hurt you?"

"I'm not injured."

What was happening then? He stepped through the door. "I don't understand. What happened in the living room?" Had she and Dave fought?

"Someone broke in."

"I know, but you've been home for hours. Why didn't you clean it up?" It would've driven her crazy to leave that mess.

"I couldn't."

"But you're not hurt."

"Right."

"Then what happened?"

"Dave left."

That was worse. Much, much worse. He sank onto the foot of her bed. "Oh."

"He met someone else. Said I'm, basically, too much trouble."

His stomach burned. The nerve of that man! "That's ridiculous."

"He's right."

"He is not right. Look at me."

When she didn't move, he got up, walked around the bed, and knelt in front of where he suspected her face was buried underneath the blankets. "Lise." He peeled back the layers.

Her red eyes and puffy lids testified to how much she'd already cried.

"Dave is an idiot. If he walked away, it isn't your fault. It's his. You are the most amazing woman I know."

"I don't think I can survive this pain, Zach. I really don't."

"Yes, you can. You are the strongest person I know too."

"You must not know very many people then." She pulled the covers back over her head. Soft sobs emanated from the bed.

Zach climbed over her legs and lay behind her, on top of the covers, and wrapped his arm around her form. "We'll get through this. Together. Just like we always have. Ever since that sandbox incident."

She chuckled.

"There. See. You can still laugh, so you'll be fine."

"This is a far cry from a little boy slinging sand in my face, Zach."

"I stood up for you then, didn't I?"

"Yes."

"I'll do the same now."

"You're a good friend, Zach."

"I know."

She jabbed him in the ribs. "Ouch. Hey, none of that now." He hugged her. "Want me to call the captain and tell him you need some time off?"

Annalise flung the covers from her head so quickly his arm flew back. "No! Cody needs me. Don't you dare."

"There's the girl I know and love."

Tears pooled in the corners of her eyes and slid silently down her cheeks.

"What is it?"

"Why can you love me for me, but my own husband thinks I'm not worth fighting for?"

"I wish I knew, Lise. I would fix it in a heartbeat for you if I could."

"Thanks." She curled under the covers again.

"Get some sleep. I'm not going anywhere."

His mind spun, reeling from thoughts of hurting Dave to wondering what he should say to help her.

But, thankfully, long minutes later, Annalise's sobs stopped, and her breathing slowed.

Tomorrow would bring a fresh wave of pain, he knew, but for now, at least, he would hold her in his arms and send all the good vibes her way he could. *Lord, please help Annalise. Give me the words and the wisdom to be a good support system for her. Give her strength and courage. And please, please help us find Cody alive.*

Chapter Twenty-Five

Annalise was greeted by the morning sun warming her cheeks. "Oh, go away." The joy the sun usually brought in mid-October was nothing but a lie today. Millie nudged her arm, and Annalise gave her the obligatory morning belly scratch. She had to face the day at some point, even if she didn't want to.

"Come on, Millie."

Annalise stopped mid-stretch. Hadn't Zach been here? Was that a dream? No, her blankets smelled like him. She threw them back and sighed. Time to face the day, whether she wanted to or not. Life wouldn't just stop for her heart breaking. Cody was still out there somewhere. Jimmy Vern too.

Expecting the living room to still be a mess, she squeezed her eyes shut as she neared the doorway. One quick peek, though, proved her wrong. Other than the duct tape covering the busted-out panel in the window and the hole in the wall, it looked exactly as it always had. Bland. No sign that her marriage even existed. It was as if her living room had known all along there was no point in decorating. No point in trying to find someone with copies of those burned wedding photographs.

Those had been the hardest thing to lose, other than their Chihuahua, Tiny. The smiles and the warmth. The sense of fulfillment and contentment she could elicit just by staring at the images of that day. She'd had no doubt Dave was the man God made for her. No reservations or even remotely chilled feet. Why, then, was she standing in her living room without him? *Lord, I don't understand. How can this be Your plan?*

Cody's mom was probably asking the same thing.

Annalise had no time for self-pity.

She followed the smell of coffee and found Zach busy at the stove. "Hey."

He spun and smiled. "Morning. Sleep well?"

"No."

"Right. Stupid question. I made breakfast."

"Thanks. It smells delicious."

"Want to go watch the interrogation this morning?"

That's just what she needed to distract herself from the issues with Dave. "Absolutely. Let me go get dressed."

"Yeah, you look horrible."

"Gee, thanks."

"I'm joking. You're beautiful, as always."

"Now I know you're lying. My eyes are puffy and red. I'm still in my clothes from yesterday."

"Nonsense. Now, go." He shooed her from the kitchen with a dish towel. "Orange French Toast and bacon will be ready when you get back."

"You're some house wife," she teased as she scooted through the doorway.

"Ha ha. Very funny."

Her smile lasted mere seconds. Too independent, huh? She certainly didn't feel self-sufficient this morning. If Zach wasn't here, she would forget to eat. If he wasn't here to distract her, she'd still be a puddle in the bed.

In the shower, she melted into a sobbing mess once more. Her salty tears mixed with the hot water as she tried to suppress her gasps so that Zach wouldn't hear. The man she loved had been with another woman. Had left their home in the darkest, loneliest hours of the morning and probably wouldn't ever come back. Her wedding vows had been shredded, stomped on, and then burned. And the part of her heart where those hopes lived felt so hollow it hurt. What was she going to do?

The water streaming over her grew colder. She shut it off robotically and dressed in the chilly bathroom, barely noticing the gooseflesh dotting her body. Was being numb normal at a time like this?

She applied a heavier-than-normal coat of makeup and crossed her fingers anyone who saw her today would assume the bloodshot eyes were from allergies or lack of sleep rather than the emotional turmoil that had poured from them for the last eight hours. She opened the door, and Zach fell backward onto the tile.

He smiled up at her. "Hi."

"What are you doing?"

"Sitting here for emotional support. I heard you crying."

Tears welled in her eyes again. God had truly blessed her when He sent Zach to the same sandbox.

"You're welcome. Let's eat." He sprang to his feet and tugged her to the kitchen.

Annalise managed to eat one piece of French toast and a few pieces of bacon, adding two cups of black coffee and hoping it was enough to keep her energy up for a few hours.

Her phone dinged with an incoming email. She opened the attachment from the sketch artist and gasped. "Look like someone we know?"

Zach took the phone. "Well, well, Jimmy Vern Buchanan."

"We have enough to question him with this."

"Yes, we do."

"Okay, interrogation first. Then pop over to give Jimmy Vern another visit?"

"Sounds like a plan to me."

Zach drove them to the Sevier County Jail and showed her to the interrogation rooms. Their arrestees hadn't been brought out yet.

Zach offered her a third cup of coffee. "I'll go find Kirk and see what's happening. You okay here?"

She smiled, but she knew it didn't reflect in her eyes. "I'm fine."

The monitor on the table in front of her blinked between two different views of the room next door. Empty, save for the table and chair.

Empty seemed to be a good theme for her morning.

As she watched the monitor, Kirk slipped into the interrogation room, slid into a chair, and folded his hands atop the table.

How did he and Zach do it? They both were so even-tempered, so calm under pressure. If she could learn half that much composure from them, she'd be happy.

The job was hers if she wanted it. Though Zach hadn't mentioned it in a day or two, she knew that it was. She squeezed her eyes shut and blew a breath through pursed lips. If Dave was removed from the equation, she could truly admit she wanted the job. More than she expected. *But it will be more cases like Cody's, won't it, Lord?*

She recognized the peace-filled voice flowing through her heart answering yes.

Could she handle that? It would be wonderful to help the families of victims that needed them the most. But what about the cases that didn't end happily? She grunted. Like this one? It sure seemed to be heading in a sour direction.

As Annalise watched the monitor, an officer stuck his head through the door and said something. Kirk leaped to his feet.

Annalise leaned in. "The sound. I can't hear the—" Who exactly was she talking to?

More importantly, why was Kirk running from the room?

The corresponding slam of the interrogation room door against the one she occupied made her jump. She raced to hers and grabbed the handle to swing it open, but it moved before she had a chance to pull.

Zach's grimace inches from her nose greeted her. "What is going on?"

Breathless, Zach grabbed her hand. "Come on."

"Zach? What is it?"

"Inmate fight. One of the men we brought in is down. Doesn't look good."

"Are you kidding me?"

He shook his head.

One look at his face and she knew he was speaking truth.

They rushed to the surveillance room and watched the chaos ensue on the many monitors there. The officers sitting at the desks in front of them spoke frazzled instructions into two separate landlines. Commands assisting their fellow comrades of each area of the prison and the inmates moving there.

Zach squeezed her hand and pointed with his other. "Look. That's Wilson on the floor there."

Her stomach turned. There was so much blood puddling around Mike Wilson's large frame. No way he was still alive. If Jimmy Vern could reach that man in prison before he had a chance to rat the Moonshine Mafia out, what else was he capable of? She needed to get everyone even remotely connected to Cody's case into protective custody. But that would be impossible.

Once she returned from the interrogation, Paul was supposed to come home with her. Maybe that wasn't such a good idea. Was that the message the intruder was leaving her? Hand over the kid who stole the money and they wouldn't do worse damage?

Well, she didn't care. They could burn that house down too. As empty as it felt, she would be glad to leave it behind in a pile of ashes. As long as no one else got hurt.

With her legs suddenly weak, Annalise sank into the closest chair and dropped her head to the desk.

She felt Zach squat beside her and place his hand on her shoulder.

"We'll get through this, Lise. All of it. Together. Remember?"

She nodded without looking up. "Once the other two hear the news, they'll never talk."

"You're probably right."

"That's encouraging."

"We'll find another way."

"It's too late, Zach. Cody's dead. He has to be after this much time has passed."

"You don't know that."

Tears ran down her nose and dripped onto the desktop. "I can't do this."

"Are we still talking about Cody?"

How did he know? She shook her head. "It hurts too much, Zach. I feel like I'm dying."

"I know."

"How?"

"My dad left me, remember?"

Of course she did.

"I was only fifteen, and he walked away. Never felt pain like that in all my life."

"I remember. I'm sorry."

"And look at me now. Handsomest devil in the Smokies."

Annalise chortled and lifted her head to stare at him. Her smile faded. He really was handsome. "Awfully full of yourself, aren't you?"

"I told you I'd never lie to you."

She laughed again. "So you did."

The frenzy on-screen had slowed down. The officers had the prisoners lined against the wall in the dining hall. A nurse hovered over the prostrate victim and shook his head.

Exactly what Annalise expected, but it was a hard reality to swallow.

Chapter Twenty-Six

The urge to keep Annalise in sight, and within grasp, almost held Zach in the monitor room, though Kirk requested his presence elsewhere. Things seemed to be under control, but what if they spiraled into a full-blown riot? Had he ever seen her looking so frail and broken? So fragile and shaky?

"Hey," he leaned in close, "I'll be right back. Do not move."

"I can take care of myself, Zach." Her muffled voice filtered through her arms and the wood of the desk, where she kept her head pressed and eyes hidden.

"I can see that."

She pointed a stern finger at the door. "Just go, you big goofball."

As soon as he cleared the door, Kirk waved to him from the end of the hall. "What's up?"

"Lockdown is going to last another hour or so. After that I'm going to go at these last two boys hard."

"Okay."

"I wouldn't hold my breath though. By the time we get them out of the general population, they will know every detail of what just happened. No doubt whoever ordered the hit will be scarier than me." He chuckled. "You know, since I have to actually follow the law and all."

Zach figured as much. "Why don't we work while we wait? Brainstorm a little?"

"Good idea. Annalise up for it too?"

"Dunno. Probably would welcome the distraction."

"What's going on with her today?"

"Not my story to tell, but she needs prayers. Bad."

"You've got it." He turned. "See you in the interrogation watch room in five."

Annalise perked up when he told her the plan, and they both made the quick walk back to meet Kirk.

He waited with an open notebook and three pens. "Let's make a map of what we know so far."

Zach grabbed a pen. "Okay, we found Buster's body in the Little Pigeon River." He jotted down the information on a sheet and tore it free. Using the magnets already in the room, he attached it to the white board and added, "In his pockets they found a Sawyer water filter."

Annalise met him at the board. "I found a gun in a little red wagon in Norris, sent it to Nashville." She put the sheet up and began another. "And then Cody was kidnapped with no real leads. His mom and dad are both cleared as suspects, for now."

"Zach and I found the bullet in the tree at the abandoned camp, postulated that was the murder scene, and sent everything for testing." Kirk handed Zach the paper he had written, and Zach added it beside the others. "Oh, and add that ballistics were a match to Annalise's gun."

"Which is what tied the two cases together." Annalise wrote Kirk's statement on the paper and then tapped the pen against her thigh. "Oh, then we found out about Paul, and I brought him into unofficial protective custody."

Zach smiled as she wrote this last bit on a new sheet and tore it free to put on the board. He loved that spark in her eye when she was puzzle-solving.

"Then my house got broken into and vandalized."

"It did?" Kirk snapped his gaze her direction.

"Yeah, and I suspect it was the kidnapper slash murderer."

"Why?"

"Because Cody stole the gun from the campsite, but Paul confessed he stole money."

Kirk grinned. "This is exactly why we need you on our team, Annalise. You connect the dots so beautifully."

Annalise blushed. "Thank you."

Zach filled in another piece of paper. "We arrested the three moonshiners, one of whom is now dead, and we probably won't get a word out of them." He sighed. "But we do know they all have Moonshine Mafia tattoos, just like Jimmy Vern and the dead man, Buster."

"We got the sketch back just a bit ago." She showed it to Kirk.

"Bears a pretty striking resemblance, I'd say."

Annalise nodded. "Yep. Do you think along with this and the missing horses, and our suspicions that they are at Jimmy Vern's, it would be enough for a warrant?" Annalise tilted her head as she studied the board.

Kirk rubbed his chin as he leaned back into his chair. "No. Even though the moonshine still was on a beeline between Cataloochee and Jimmy Vern's house, there is too much coincidence and not enough hard evidence."

"When Annalise and I interviewed him, he was slick as a snake. If he truly is the one behind the murder, the moonshine, the kidnapping, and now the hit on Wilson, he isn't going to talk either."

"Gee, good optimism, Zach." Annalise rolled her eyes. "You never know, once we get out of here, maybe he will give us something."

Silence filled the room. She was getting her hopes up too much.

Kirk rose and began pacing the rear of the room. "What are we missing?"

Zach studied Annalise while she studied the sheets. Her intensity radiated in almost palpable waves. This was good for her. And there was no doubt she was in her element. Was he wrong in wanting to protect her from the SMIF team and its inherent risks? Clearly, she thrived on situations like these.

"Oh, we have the receipt for the water filters. We can stop by Bass Pro Shops on the way to Jimmy Vern's and see if they'll show us the videos." She snapped the lid on and off the marker. "The money." Annalise spun. "Paul said he spent it all. He told me some things, but they would only total up to maybe $1500. Is that worth Jimmy Vern risking his entire empire over?"

Zach shook his head. "You wouldn't think so."

"Fifteen hundred would be a drop in the hat for a man like Buchanan. No way. Annalise, we need to talk to Paul again."

She nodded. "As soon as this lockdown—"

The door swung open, and an officer stuck his head in. "Y'all can go now."

Zach smiled. "Perfect timing."

He was going to die in this stinking hole, and his mom and dad would never know what became of him.

Cody no longer had the energy to try to sit up and no longer had the moisture to cry any tears, though he wanted to.

God? I've never been much on talking to You, and I'm sorry about that. I need to ask You for a favor. Please watch over my mom. Help her get through this. Tell her somehow I'm sorry and I love her.

He watched helplessly as his beloved daily sunbeam shone, changing angles with each passing minute, and then moved on. He wouldn't ever feel the sunshine again. Or taste his mom's homemade tacos or chocolate milkshakes or anything else for that matter. He'd never get to go to school again. Ha. Get to. He'd never thought of school in those terms before.

But more than anything, the fact that he would never get to say those words to his mother burned inside his heart. She had worked so hard to take care of him and keep everything going when Dad left, and all he'd repaid her with was snarky teenage attitude and bad grades. If only he could go back and fix it all.

It was too late. Jimmy Vern had him stashed somewhere good, apparently, and no one was coming to his rescue.

They had gone from zero leads to so many that Annalise wasn't sure which was the best to follow first. All of them tugged at her. Though she longed to speak with Jimmy Vern, it did make sense to take the time and stop at Bass Pro Shops on the way.

"We need to speak to the manager on duty, please," Annalise said and showed her badge. "It's urgent."

The young cashier's face paled. "Sure, um, hang on a sec." She paged someone on the phone and just a few minutes later, a thick gentleman sporting a fisherman's vest and hat approached. Interesting get up.

"Sorry, I model some of the sale items for the day. This way, the men see how functional it is, even if they never make it to the fishing department." He rubbed his hands together. "So, how may I help you?"

Zach spoke first. "We have a person of interest in custody, possibly involved in a disappearance. We were hoping to check video feeds."

Annalise handed him the receipt.

The manager studied it and then shook his head. "I'm sorry. The feed is on a loop. If we have no incidences for the month prior, they are recorded over. The feed you're requesting no longer exists."

Her breath caught.

"Thanks for your time." Zach directed her outside. "Hey, we still have the sketch, and Kirk just sent me a still-shot from the gas station. Unfortunately, all we got is plates. No image of him. But the truck for sure belongs to Jimmy Vern. The little mom and pop store's video cameras are mostly for show, but maybe we will get lucky and he'll slip up when we go see him."

She nodded. Zach was right. There was still reason to hope, at least the little bit she'd allowed to pop back up this morning. All of the new leads couldn't come up empty, could they?

Zach aimed the truck toward Pigeon Forge.

Gatlinburg lay just beyond. Was Dave there now? With his mistress? Nausea stirred her stomach to life. She had to find a way to squelch the images of him and her together, before they took full shape and made her actually vomit. How had life gotten to this point?

"You okay over there?"

She snapped her gaze toward Zach and forced a smile. "Yeah. I'm fine."

"No, you're not. And it's okay. You've been through an awful lot of emotional stuff the last couple days."

"Yeah."

"Why did the chicken cross the road?"

"Huh?"

"To prove to the possum it could be done."

Despite herself, she chuckled. "Thanks, Zach."

"Anytime."

Several quiet miles later, he turned into Jimmy Vern's driveway and parked in the same spot as before. The same dogs came scrambling out to bark and bite at their tires.

Jimmy Vern stepped onto the porch. He didn't call the dogs back this time.

Zach rolled his window down as far as he dared with the Rottweiler on his door. "We need to talk, Jimmy Vern."

"Ain't got nothing to say to you two."

"We've got enough to bring you in for questioning. It's your decision. Here or at the station."

Jimmy Vern looped his fingers through his overall straps and then whistled. The dogs retreated.

Zach and Annalise stepped out together. Her first few tentative steps, she thought the Rottweiler eyeballing her was sure to charge. She sighed when he didn't.

"Officer Baker needs to show you something, Jimmy Vern."

Annalise pulled the photo from the envelope and held it up. "This is a sketch from an eyewitness who saw you at a gas station in Maryville the night Cody Moss was kidnapped."

Jimmy Vern glanced at the image. "Ain't me. Dunno what to tell ya."

Zach pulled the new photo up on his phone and showed it to Jimmy Vern. "Really? 'Cause this is your truck, isn't it? With your license plate number. Quite a coincidence wouldn't you say, Officer Baker?"

Annalise held back her smirk. "Yep. Sure is."

"So what if I was there? Needed gas."

"Who was with you?" Zach pressed.

Jimmy Vern grinned. "I had Jack and Daniels with me." He pointed toward the boards under his feet. "It's all coming back to me now."

Oh, yeah right. Of course his dogs were named after the most infamous Tennessee liquor ever.

"Glad to see your memory is nice and healthy there, Jimmy Vern." Zach crossed his arms over his chest. "Anything else you'd like to add?"

"Nope."

Zach turned toward the truck, stopped, and leaned on the hood. "You wouldn't know anything about that still we busted over the mountain, would you?"

Jimmy Vern opened his mouth but closed it and shook his head.

Figured. No one was talking. No one was willing to save Cody. Brittle hope burst inside her. If only she could cross the line and look in that barn without some stupid piece of paper. Or pin Jimmy Vern to the side of the house and force him to speak.

"We will be back, Jimmy Vern," she said through clenched teeth. "It's just a matter of time."

Jimmy Vern spat.

It ripped her heart out to get back into the truck and head for home empty-handed. Was Cody here somewhere? Could he hear them? *Lord, this is torture! Help Cody stay strong, wherever he is.*

"What do we do now, Zach?"

"We'll get him. I'm more convinced than ever he's guilty. Of everything."

She was too, but they had to have concrete proof if they were going to nail him. And that kind of solidity seemed awfully scarce. In any part of her world lately.

Chapter Twenty-Seven

I75 North zipped by Zach's car. If Annalise focused on the immediate tasks at hand and Zach's speed, she didn't think—as much—about Cody or Dave. The ache throbbed rather than pierced, for the moment.

Her phone rang, and she picked up the call on the first ring. "Captain Brooks, thanks for calling me back."

"Sure thing. What's up?"

"One of the arrested men, Mike Wilson, was murdered on his way to the interrogation room at the jail earlier."

"Oh, man."

"Yeah, we were really hoping to crack one of these guys. Seems impossible now, but we left Kirk with the remaining two living ones. Pray for a miracle."

"I will."

She updated him on the photos and conversation with Jimmy Vern. "I need to speak with Paul as soon as we get back, in about thirty minutes."

"He's here. Settled in real nice, Annalise. I gotta say, I like the boy."

"That is a lot coming from you, sir. You're a great judge of character."

Annalise hung up.

Zach barely slowed for the right turn at the exit.

"Good thing the light was green."

"Huh?" He glanced in his mirror. "Oh, right."

"You okay?"

"Just thinkin'."

"About what?"

"A lot's happened the last few days."

No kidding. But she didn't want to rehash all of it. Not right now when her mind felt like waves on a windy day rather than during a hurricane. "Swing by real quick and let me check on Celine."

Zach nodded and a few minutes later pulled up to the curb in front of the Moss home.

"I'll be right back." Annalise bounded up the front steps and knocked on the bright blue door. "Celine?"

When there was no answer, she went to the back door and repeated her actions. She tried the handle and found it open. "Celine?" she called once more from the open rear entryway.

The quiet house sent goosebumps racing up her arms. She pulled her gun from her hip holster and crept through the kitchen and dining room, and stepped over the threshold into the living room. Why was it so dark in the middle of the afternoon? The curtains pulled over the windows allowed little sunlight to enter. And no lamps lit the space at all.

Her breaths felt shallow and heavy as she made her way up the stairs and into the first open door on the right.

A trail of red dotted the plush carpet. Annalise's heart sank. She texted Zach, "Need backup," and slid along the wall. The queen-sized bed was empty, and a pair of pink slippers waited under the edge. Where was Celine?

The trail led into the bathroom off the master bedroom. Annalise nudged the door. Something blocked it from the inside. *Lord, I have such a bad feeling. Help me, please.*

Annalise didn't want to push too hard and hurt Celine, if she was in fact the obstruction. She pushed gently, held her breath, and squeezed through the narrow opening.

As she feared, Celine lay in a motionless heap behind the door.

Annalise held her breath as she knelt and watched for the rise and fall of Celine's chest.

"Where are you?" Zach's voice sounded from the hallway.

"In here! Call 9-1-1." She felt Celine's slow pulse and sighed. At least she was still breathing, and her heart was beating. But, beyond that, Annalise wasn't sure she could say anything positive. Celine's swollen face would've been unrecognizable had Annalise not known this was for sure her form lying on the floor. How long had she been like this?

Blood pooled beneath her head, a nosebleed that seemed to be slowing to a drip. The crooked bone on the bridge proof of its broken state.

"Annalise?" Zach shouted and then knocked on the door.

"She's right behind the door, don't push."

"Are you okay?"

"I'm fine. I haven't cleared the rest of the house, though. Can you please make sure we are alone?"

"Yes. Stay put."

Like she had any choice. "Oh, Celine. What happened to you?" Even as she whispered the words, she had a sinking feeling she knew the answer. Jimmy Vern Buchanan.

Her heartbeat quickened. If he had broken into Annalise's house and come after Celine in her own home, was Paul safe anywhere?

She heard Zach's footsteps approaching the door once again. "Everything okay?"

"Seems to be. Can I help?"

"I don't think there's much we can do. She's stable but unconscious. Someone has beaten her to a pulp."

Zach growled. "Jimmy Vern."

"That's what I was thinking too."

"We need to dust for fingerprints. I know there weren't any in Cody's room, or your house, but maybe he got careless this time."

"One can only hope." But she doubted it. Jimmy Vern knew exactly what not to do. His first arrest had given him quite the felon's education.

"I'll get started out here on the doorknobs. Oh, and I think the fight started in the office. There's a lot of blood there."

Celine must've tried to make it to her bathroom to clean up after the pummeling and passed out. Why hadn't she called the police or gone to the ER?

The wail of sirens pierced the walls and reached her. Oh, thank goodness.

Chapter Twenty-Eight

The ambulance pulled out of the driveway, Annalise riding alongside Celine. He would pick her up later. After he finished processing the house.

A text from Kirk lit up his cellphone screen.

"Got nothing from these two. Figured as much. Guess my impeccable record is going to have to take a hit, eh?"

"Nah. Your hands were tied on this one. Won't count." Zach sighed and then sent a second message. "Celine Moss has been attacked. I'm going over the scene with a fine-toothed comb. I'll call later and update."

Zach resumed his investigation in the study. So far, he'd fingerprinted all the door handles throughout the entire house and collected samples to compare, again, with everyone they knew had been coming and going the last few days. He didn't have high hopes of getting lucky.

He had photographed and collected blood samples from the trail leading to the bedroom and from the bathroom where Annalise had found Celine. He suspected it all belonged to Celine. When he had finally seen her, it had taken his breath. And not in a good way. How could someone do that to a woman?

The office was something straight out of a Stephen King novel. He hardly knew where to begin. Which blood spatter puddle was the most important? He squatted over the largest one on the floor and tilted his head. His pulse skipped. Was that a boot print? This could be the most helpful thing they'd found so far.

He enhanced the shoe print and lifted it, carefully preserving the details for the lab. If they could match this print to a particular brand, to a specific store, maybe they'd get lucky and find video proof of the purchaser. It was a long shot, but if it worked, they would have fail-proof evidence of Jimmy Vern's involvement.

He probably shouldn't be narrowed into one suspect yet, but if it wasn't Jimmy Vern behind all of this, he'd eat his own boot.

Zach packed up his gear and made his way to the truck. He hated to leave the place in such a terrible state, but he wouldn't be able to clear the scene for clean-up just yet.

He swung by Annalise's house. Nothing seemed out of place there. Dave's truck was still absent. Was that a good thing or a bad? Zach wanted to beat some sense into the man, but at the same time, would it be healthy for Annalise if Dave decided to fight for their marriage? All he wanted was for her to be happy. As much as she loved Dave, and was committed to her marriage vows, if he'd cheated once, what was stopping him from doing it again? Zach growled. Nothing, that's what.

Zach couldn't stand cheaters. They hurt the women they loved for temporary reprieve, love, pleasure, whatever. And left a web of destruction and chaos behind them. Broken families. Broken hearts. Broken dreams.

He knew all too well how little Cody Moss felt. Annalise didn't deserve this kind of pain.

Annalise tapped her toes on the linoleum floor. She really needed to get home, to check on Paul. Captain Brooks had assured her he was holed up in the extra bedroom at the Brooks' residence. All was quiet on the home front. Why, then, did the nagging fear clawing at her mind cease to leave her?

Celine lay in the bed to Annalise's left. The CT scan came back surprisingly clear, but the next twenty-four to forty-eight hours would be critical. If her brain began to swell …

Why was it that her life of late was counted in hours? In critical, tick-tock, life-is-draining, chances-of-success-are-dwindling-with-each-passing-one hours?

Celine had needed a blood transfusion and was heavily sedated. With a broken nose, left collar bone, and left wrist, Annalise hoped they kept the poor woman that way for a while yet. Something kept Annalise by her side, though she couldn't get any pertinent details from an unconscious woman. She couldn't just leave her alone. Would Brian want to know? Would it be a good idea for him to be here, after the huge fight Annalise had witnessed?

She dropped her head to the corner of the bed. If she was here, she wasn't out trying to find their son. *Lord, help!*

Celine wouldn't care about her own health. She would want Annalise to be doing everything within her power to find her boy. If it wasn't too late already.

Annalise shot to her feet. In the hallway, she flagged down a nurse. "I need to know as soon as Ms. Moss wakes. I have very important questions for her." She handed the nodding, wide-eyed nurse a business card. "Please call me the minute she opens her eyes. Okay?"

"Yes, Officer. I will"

She called Zach on the way to her truck. "What'd you find?"

"Blood. Lots of it. Did Celine have any other injuries? Stab wounds or anything?"

"No. not that I am aware of."

"Why on earth was there so much blood?"

Annalise bit her lip. "What if it is the attacker's blood too? Did you find evidence that Celine fought back?'

"No. I collected a bunch of different blood samples, maybe we will get lucky."

"Maybe. What else?"

"A partial boot print."

Her eyebrow shot up. "That could be a good lead."

"Could be. What's the plan? You staying at the hospital?"

"I'm leaving now. I need to talk to Paul. And check on Brian and update him."

"I'll get these samples to the lab and then join you wherever you are. Keep me posted."

"Will do." She took a deep breath. "Thanks for … everything, Zach."

"No thanks needed."

"I'll cook you a really big dinner when this is all over."

"I won't say no to that."

She chuckled. "I know you won't. It's a pretty safe bet to offer you food." As they had grown and she had gotten married, their friendship had changed. It was still good, of course. But instead of confiding in him, she'd spent years confiding in Dave. As it should be. She had missed Zach and not been able to explain it fully to herself or Dave just how much. "You're important to me, Zach."

Silence filled the air between them for many seconds. "You are to me too, Annalise."

He was her first best friend, not to mention her longest friendship. She would never take him for granted again. "All right, I'll call you in a bit."

She knocked on Brian's hotel room door.

Something on the other side crashed to the floor.

She drew her gun and stepped to the side, her heart climbing into her throat. "Brian? You okay?" She jiggled the handle and found it locked. "I'm coming in five, four, three—"

The door swung open. Brian lurched into view. "What?"

"Are you drunk?"

"Might be. What's it to you?"

Was this a theme with the men around her or something? "I ... Or ..." She took a deep breath and pushed thoughts of Dave back behind the curtain. "Celine has been attacked."

His shining eyes widened. "What? Is she okay?"

"She is in the hospital, under heavy sedation. She has a lot of broken bones, but the doctors are optimistic she will be okay. As long as her brain doesn't begin to swell."

He stumbled backward into the door frame and wiped his hand across his brow. "I have to get to her."

"You cannot drive in your condition. Nor would you be any help at the hospital."

"What about Cody? Have you figured anything more out?"

She swallowed hard. "We are currently following a lead, but I would advise you not to get your hopes up." Hers were certainly sinking by the hour.

"I need to get home."

What?

"My wife needs me home." He backed into the room.

Annalise followed.

He sank onto the bed and hung his head between his hands. "But I can't leave either." He sighed. "This is all my fault."

Annalise wanted to argue with him, but she couldn't bring herself to do it. It kind of was his fault. He'd abandoned his family and driven Cody to rebel.

He raised a tear-streaked face toward her. "I don't know what to do. I feel so helpless holed up in this dumb hotel room. At least at home, I'll be with my family."

She clenched her fists. His family? His other family, more correctly. Had he not cared about Celine and Cody at all? Was it so easy to toss them aside? To flush his marriage down the drain and walk away with the mistress he never should've had in the first place? "How dare you! Are you all the same?" Tears sprang to her eyes.

Brian recoiled. "I—"

"Don't bother. There's something about husbands, isn't there? Some ridiculous, unspoken rule that says, 'You get bored with one, go ahead and move on to the next.' It's disgusting."

Red crept up his neck and colored his cheeks. He sprang from the bed. "What do you know about my life? Huh? Your job is to find my son, and you can't even do that." He turned his back. "Get out, before I call real police. The ones who know how to help people."

With her chest tight and tears streaming down her face, Annalise backed from the room and ran to her vehicle through a cold October drizzle.

Something little, with annoying buzzing wings landed on Cody's forearm. He peeled open sticky eyelids and stared at his injured hand. He couldn't see a thing, but the sound of the little wings clued him in to the bug's identity. "I'm not dead yet, stupid fly." How could it take so much effort just to brush one small bug away?

His hip bones and ribs ached. He'd lost track of how long he'd been lying in the same position. Leftover dreams turned nightmares clouded his thoughts. One minute he was home, the next buried alive. One minute eating pizza, the next his stomach cramped and tore his abdomen open. Stupid subconscious, or wherever dreams came from.

What was that new sound? He arched his neck and listened. Water? Water! Dripping through the walls somewhere behind him. His parched mouth and sandpaper tongue overpowered all his other body parts. He pulled his knees to his chest and rolled. His arms shook as he lifted himself to a crawling position. Seriously. How could he be so weak? Had Jimmy Vern done something to that chicken he'd offered? Some sort of slow-acting poison?

The painstaking effort it took to crawl to the trickle made Cody's chest heave, but he finally felt the cool drips sliding down the rocks. He pressed his lips to it and groaned. He never dreamed cold, clear water could be so delicious.

What if he got sick? He pulled back and swiped his mouth with a shaking hand. Oh, right. He already was. He chuckled, ending in a cough that pulled down to the very bottom of his lungs. Fantastic.

The cellar door slammed open, and Cody jumped.

"Hey, boy! Where you at?"

He didn't want to answer, wasn't sure he could the way his mouth still clove together.

"Boy? Your momma says hi." Jimmy Vern's hoarse laugh filled the damp space. "Actually, she couldn't really say much at all after I finished with her."

"You leave my mom alone!" What had Jimmy Vern done to her? Tears sprang to his eyes. Was she going to be okay?

Jimmy Vern approached, hovering in a shadow behind his flashlight. "What's wrong with you?"

Oh, where should Cody begin? He bit his tongue to keep the sarcasm from spilling over. "I'm sick."

The flashlight blinded him as Jimmy Vern turned it Cody's direction.

"You look awful. Here," he threw a jug of water at him, "drink somethin'."

Cody didn't reach for it.

"It'll make you feel better." Jimmy Vern squatted. "Your mom couldn't tell me where Paul was either. I will go back, if you don't." He pulled his cell phone out and flipped to a picture of Cody's mom.

Cody's stomach roiled. He turned his head and vomited the water he'd just managed to drink. Her bloodied, swollen face might have been the most awful thing Cody had ever seen. "What? Why—"

"Where is Paul?"

"How am I supposed to know? You've kept me in this hole for over three days. He could be anywhere."

Jimmy Vern chuckled. "Four days, kid. Where does he usually live?"

"Out on Highway 61." Cody didn't have the energy to try to resist anymore. What did it matter? Paul had brought this monster down on his own back and gotten Cody's mom beaten up.

"Good boy. Drink up. When I find Paul, I'll bring more food. When I find my money, you can go."

"Yeah, right. Just go ahead and kill me and get it over with."

"Don't tempt me."

Cody didn't care too much what happened to him. "Just leave my mom alone."

"Scout's honor." Jimmy Vern's disgusting laugh faded behind him as he left Cody alone in the dark once again.

He unscrewed the lid and took a swig. It burned all the way down. He choked and labored to catch his breath. Figured the jerk would leave him whiskey instead of water. He'd seen men on old Westerns use whiskey to sterilize wounds. Maybe he should try it.

He poured a stream onto his hand. If he'd thought it burned going down his throat, he was wrong. He stifled a scream, biting his lip instead. And then took another long swig to ease the throbbing ache.

Cody curled into a ball, with his mouth beneath the water and drank as much as he could. *God, if You're there please help my mom. I don't want Jimmy Vern to find Paul, not really, but I want this to be over. Can't You just take me home now?*

He'd never thought much about Heaven one way or another. But he imagined it would be a sweet home. Beautiful, peaceful, and painless. Safe. A place without fear or bad men like Jimmy Vern. Cody drifted to sleep, imaging his mother's sweet face.

Chapter Twenty-Nine

"Have you been crying?" Captain Brooks scrutinized her face.

She dipped her head. "I'm fine. Is Paul ready to go home?" The word home didn't quite seem fitting anymore, but what else should she call it? The shell where her life used to be normal? The place where she'd hoped to grow old with a man who decided she was too much trouble? She sighed. "I don't want to talk about it."

"Paul!" Captain Brooks shouted up the stairs. He turned back to face her. "What's going on?"

"It's personal." She fiddled with her key fob.

"Ah, enough said." He held up his hands. "How is Celine?"

"She was still out of it when I left."

"Probably good, all things considered." He squeezed her shoulder. "We're going to get them, Annalise. No matter how long it takes."

"That's what I'm afraid of. Cody can't possibly make it much longer."

"You don't know that."

"Right. Think Paul heard you?"

Captain Brooks chuckled. "I'm not sure how he couldn't. Hang on, I'll go check."

Annalise waited at the bottom of the steps, her mind tracking from one bad thing to another. It seemed she couldn't find a single positive to land and focus on.

Captain Brooks thudded down the stairs.

She spun and felt the blood drain from her face. "What is it?"

"He's gone."

"Gone? How can he be gone?"

"I...I don't know. He didn't go by me. Only thing I can figure is he went out the window onto the porch roof and jumped off."

Her heart sank to her stomach. This wasn't good. Jimmy Vern was hurting people left and right. What if he'd already gotten to Paul? "Are you sure he wasn't...taken?"

"I can't be sure." His voice shook. "I'm so sorry, Annalise. I wasn't...I don't know how this happened."

She placed her hand on his arm. "It's not your fault, Captain." How she wanted to be angry with him! To blame the man standing right in front of her instead of the one who seemed invincible and invisible behind all this violence. But she couldn't.

She'd already blown up on Brian for no reason. She wasn't going to do it to Milt too.

While Captain Brooks whipped out his phone and barked orders for an APB, increased patrols, and an Amber Alert, Annalise called Zach. "Paul's missing."

"Oh, Annalise. I'm so sorry." He sighed. "I just dropped off the samples. I'm on my way."

"Meet me at Paul and his brother's house." Why hadn't she tried harder to find Paul's brother? It hadn't seemed pertinent to her case, but now she wished she could speak with him. Maybe he would know Paul's go-to places to hide. She dialed the number she'd gotten from Cathy a few days ago. It had been disconnected. Oh, just great.

"We need to add an APB for Paul's brother Orrin too, Captain."

He nodded and added the directive to the list he was giving.

What if Paul wasn't hiding? If Jimmy Vern had gotten to him too...

Her chest muscles constricted, forcing her breaths to grow shallow. She clutched her chest and bent over, sudden dizziness claiming her. This had gone too far. Too many innocent people were getting railroaded and run over. *Lord, I'm at a loss. I don't know what to do!*

Captain Brooks's strong hand pressed her back. "Pull it together, Officer. We've got work to do."

He was right, but her bootstraps were so far away.

"You can do this, Annalise. You're the strongest person I know."

"I…can't…breathe."

He rubbed her back. "Try to take one deep breath."

She drew in as much air as she could.

"Good. Now another."

The second one was deeper and slowed her heart rate more.

"This isn't about the case, is it?"

The compassion in his voice drew her tears. She shook her head. "Dave left me."

Before she knew what was happening, Captain Brooks drew her into his arms and held her close. "I've been there. It's a terrible feeling."

She nodded and wiped her tears.

"It will get better, I promise. I know it doesn't feel like it right now, but it will."

She attempted a smile. "Thanks."

"We have a teenager to find. And once we do, he is grounded for the rest of his life."

"We aren't even his parents."

"Don't care. He's grounded. That's final."

"Do you—" She couldn't finish the sentence and ruin the idea. Not yet. Did Captain Brooks wish Paul was his son? Would he be willing to foster and then adopt the boy, if it became an option? She smiled.

"What?"

"Nothing. Come on."

She followed Captain Brooks to Paul's house. There didn't appear to be anyone home, but as they entered the front door, she realized someone had been here. The mess was even worse than before. Had his brother done that? Or had Jimmy Vern been looking for his money and torn the place to pieces? The nappy couch cushions had been shredded, the few photos on the wall thrown to the floor, and every cupboard opened and emptied. Fragments of dishes and glasses littered the counters and tile, and the fridge stood open, warm air already having fought out the cold. From the look of the leftover pizza, a while ago.

Annalise wrinkled her nose. "Do you smell that?"

Captain Brooks paused his search of the living room. "Is that smoke?"

"Where's it coming from?" She whipped her gaze to the oven. None of the knobs were turned on.

"Back here." Captain Brooks walked down the narrow hallway.

Annalise followed, her heart climbing into her throat. "Paul!" There was no response. She checked the room closest, while Captain Brooks ducked into the next open doorway. The bedroom had been ransacked too, but Paul was not here.

"Fire!" Captain Brooks's voice boomed from somewhere deeper in the house.

Fire? Seriously? She stepped through the door and collided with the captain.

"Out, Annalise. Now!"

He grabbed her arm and dragged her through the front door. She glanced back in time to see a wall of flames burst out after them. A loud pop and a whooshing roar soared over their heads as she forced her wobbly legs to clamber down the porch steps. She didn't stop running until she reached her truck at the curb.

Captain Brooks leaned on the hood next to her, doubled over, coughing.

"What. Was. That?"

"Some sort of slow-burning fuse led into a jug of something. Possibly kerosene."

"Or moonshine?"

Captain Brooks groaned. "Possibly." He grabbed his shoulder mic and requested the fire department, followed by another round of coughing.

"You okay?"

"Yeah. I pushed that back bedroom door open and a wall of smoke poured over top of me. Musta took a big breath or something."

They backed their vehicles to what she hoped was a safe distance and watched helplessly as the flames licked the window and door frames. She would have thought the cold rain streaming from the sky would help, but the fire burned so hot, the water hissed as it evaporated, almost as loud as the flames. The last time she watched a house burn down, it was her own. She shuddered. Nothing about this line of work was easy. Did finding lost boys and taking down bad guys make moments like these worth it?

Yes.

Except when she failed at it.

Ten minutes later, the squalling fire truck pulled into the driveway, just as the roof collapsed.

"Not much to save." Had Jimmy Vern found his money? No doubt he'd cleared the house before he'd torched it. And there would be no returning the game system for a refund now. What was she talking about? If they found the money, it was state's evidence and would never be returned to Jimmy Vern.

She shouldn't be jumping to conclusions. There was still no hard evidence of Jimmy Vern's guilt. And she knew better, but the idea of anyone besides Buchanan being responsible sure didn't sit well. He was guilty. They just had to find a way to prove what her gut already knew.

The sun crept toward the horizon as the men fought to put out the blaze. By the time the fire smoldered to black ashes, there was not much left. She knew all too well what that looked like and felt like.

A bobbing glow in the back woods caught Annalise's eye. What on earth? She tapped Captain Brooks on the elbow and signaled.

"On your lead, Baker."

Her weapon drawn, she took much the same route she had the other night and cautiously approached the trees. The light flicked off. "Paul, I know it's you." She was taking a gamble here. She held her breath. *Lord, let it be him please.* "Don't run. We are worried about you."

The silence pressed in so heavily, she could scarcely breathe. What if it was Jimmy Vern, out there in the dark taking aim for her head?

"I know there's more money than you told me. As long as you keep trying to hide it, you're in danger."

A rustle in the leaves sounded a bit closer than before.

"And you're signing Cody's death certificate."

"Fine."

Annalise jumped at the sound of Paul's voice nearby. She spun and shined her flashlight into the inky darkness.

Paul stepped from a tree not five feet from her.

Behind her, Captain Brooks sighed. "Glad to see you're okay, boy."

"Paul, listen to me."

Paul met her eyes.

"Tell me where the money is. It's our last hope of bringing him home alive."

"I overheard the captain on the phone. If that guy attacked Cody's mom so bad, what's to say Cody's still breathing?"

He had a good point. *Lord?* "Nothing. But I have hope." Sort of. There was just enough left in the drying well to keep her going.

"If I give him back his cash, you really think he'll let Cody go and leave me alone?"

It sounded ridiculous spoken aloud, but there wasn't much else left to do. "We have to try."

Paul dipped his chin. "Come on."

Captain Brooks followed on her heels while Paul led them farther into the forest. She should have known he would have hidden the stash out here. Maybe for a scared teenager with a jerky, incompetent brother as his caretaker, invisibility in the dark woods felt safer than home.

Paul led them to the creek's edge, still swollen with the rains, and squatted next to an old stump. He pulled a large, black backpack from its hollowed out base. "Here. Ten thousand big ones."

Annalise's heart nearly stopped. "Are you serious?"

He nodded.

No wonder the kid had wanted to keep the money. It meant a new lease on life for him. And no wonder Jimmy Vern wanted it back.

Chapter Thirty

Zach could see the glow on the underside of the dark clouds long before he reached Paul's house. The sinking feeling in his gut accompanied the instant thought of fire. And he instinctively knew it was at his destination.

He rounded the last bend and pulled to the curb next to Annalise's truck. "What happened? Is Paul hurt?"

Annalise smiled. "Glad you could make it, slow poke. But, no, Paul's fine." She pointed to her back seat, obscured by her dark windows.

He could just barely see the outline of a head and shoulders in the rear. "Good. How did the fire start?"

Captain Brooks rubbed a hand over his stubbly chin. "Some sort of accelerant in a jug. Possibly whiskey."

Zach clamped down a sarcastic chuckle. "Of course. Why did I even have to ask?"

Annalise elbowed him. "It was out, but they've had another flare up. I can't imagine what is left to burn."

She had a good point. Maybe just the carpet and floor, and the few pieces of furniture illuminated by the glow. "I'm glad no one's hurt."

"Me too. The captain and I had a bit of a close call."

He swallowed hard.

Annalise placed a hand on his forearm. "I'm fine. I promise."

He managed to nod. "What now?"

"We've got the money. And a bargaining chip."

"What's your plan?"

"Let's visit Celine first, and I'll tell you on the way."

She opened her back door. "Paul, you need to stay with Captain Brooks a little longer."

Zach heard him mumble something.

"You will stay put this time, mister. You understand me?"

"Yes, ma'am."

Paul slinked from Annalise's vehicle and got into the passenger seat of Captain Brooks's.

"I'll duct tape him to the stair rails if I have to this time, Annalise." Captain Brooks chuckled.

"I don't think that will be necessary, sir. I bet he's not going anywhere this time."

Annalise spun and grabbed Zach by the elbow. "Let's go."

He dropped his truck off in Annalise's driveway and climbed into hers. Forty-five minutes later, they pulled into the University of Tennessee Medical Center and wound their way up to Celine's new room.

Annalise stopped in the doorway, and Zach crashed into her back. She stood riveted, open mouthed. "What? What's wrong?"

"Nothing. She's awake."

He peeked around the door frame.

A much-bruised-but-smiling Celine waved at him. "So good to see you ali—awake, Ms. Moss."

She giggled. "I'm glad I'm alive too, Officer Leebow. Thank you."

"Forgive me if it is none of my business, but you seem so at peace, Celine." Annalise pulled a chair up and sat next to the bed.

"I had a dream you found my Cody. I think it was a sign from God."

Zach's pulse skipped. What must Annalise be thinking? He had serious doubts about Cody's health and safety by this point. He had been in the kidnapper's custody far too long.

"Ms. Moss, I...um, please don't get your hopes up too high." Annalise's voice hitched. "I really am trying my best, but it's been nearly five days. The odds of him coming home alive are, well, not great."

Celine's face paled, but she patted Annalise's hand and smiled. "I have hope."

Zach crossed his arms over his chest, his gaze glued to Annalise's face. He could read the emotions crossing there like an open diary. She had hope, too, but it was wavering and ringed with a thick dose of fear and doubt. Not to mention self-criticism and a broken heart.

"Celine, I…" She dropped her head. "I'll do my best."

"Officer Leebow, would you pray with us?"

He jerked his gaze to Ms. Moss's. "I…um, of course." He stepped forward and took their hands. "Lord, please help Ms. Moss continue to heal, with no residual effects from the injuries she sustained. Above all else, please watch over Cody, wherever he is right now, and help us bring him home, safe." His thudding heart began to slow with a new peace. "Lead us to the man responsible and let him face justice. Strengthen Mr. and Ms. Moss while they wait for You to answer their prayers. Amen."

Celine squeezed his hand, and he opened his eyes.

"Thank you." Tears shone in the corners of Celine's eyes. "Bring my baby home to me, please."

All he could manage was an unsteady nod. What if they failed? What if they found a body instead of a breathing boy?

Annalise cleared her throat. "How are you? What are the doctors saying about your recovery?"

"Still have all these broken bones." Celine chuckled. "But my brain imaging seems to be normal."

"That's wonderful. Can you remember anything about the attack?"

"I have some vague blips that come up in my dreams. I know it was a man. Average height."

A nurse entered the room. "Oh, Officer Baker, good. I was just trying to phone you. Ms. Moss is awake." She smiled at him and turned away. "I guess you can see that." She checked Ms. Moss's vitals. "Do you need anything?"

"No, thank you." Celine smiled.

The nurse caught his eye briefly as she passed, and a quick blush spread up her cheeks. Too bad he wasn't interested. She seemed sweet, and she was certainly attractive. The blush told him she was thinking the same thing, but he didn't need a new relationship right now. Not with Annalise's situation. He wouldn't be able to focus on helping her if he was distracted by a beautiful brunette with big, brown eyes and—No. He forced his attention back to the women's conversation.

"He wore a mask, I think. One of those generic ski masks, if my nightmares are accurate. He kept asking me about money, but I had no idea what he was talking about."

"He clearly didn't believe you," Annalise said.

"No. Then he asked me about Paul, I think. I must have passed out, because I don't remember him leaving. I woke sometime later on the office floor and stumbled upstairs. I needed to clean myself up."

"You needed to call 9-1-1," Zach said.

"Yes, I suppose that's true. But all I could think was, 'I must look a sight.' Next thing I remember, I woke up here."

"Why did you bleed so much, Celine? Were there other injuries I didn't find?"

"I'm on blood thinners for a blood clot in my leg we found last spring."

"And you're okay from that too?" Concern wrinkled Annalise's brow.

Celine nodded. "I'm lucky. No, scratch that. I'm blessed."

Annalise smiled. "I admire your outlook on everything."

Was she thinking about her own everything? He longed to pull her into his arms and remind her that she was strong, beautiful, and resilient. To convince her everything would be okay. *Lord, reassurance like that can only come from You. Help me help her. Show me what to do and say.*

Annalise said her goodbyes, and they drove to the closest Waffle House for a three a.m. meal. His idea. "All right. Spill it. What are you thinking here?"

Her gaze darted to the truck.

"Did you bring the money?"

She nodded.

"That's evidence, Annalise. It should have been locked at the station, or we could take it to Kirk."

"It's our only bargaining chip, Zach."

"It's a good way to lose our bargaining chip and our lives, Annalise." He pinned her with his most serious glare. "I'm calling Kirk."

"No." She grabbed his wrist and smiled. "Just hang on a sec. Let me tell you my thoughts, and then we can call him and get his help too. We will need as much wit as we can find."

"We can't march in there without a warrant, Annalise."

She dropped her chin, some of the fight leaving her eyes. "I know."

"We need evidence. Something to concretely tie Jimmy Vern to everything."

"Have you heard anything about the boot print yet?"

"It's only been a few hours, and they were leaving for the night when I dropped off the sample."

"Oh, right."

"I tell you what. Come crash on my couch for the rest of the short night we have left. First thing in the morning, we'll go stare at the forensics team until they finish."

She chuckled. "Okay. You win."

"Good. I am a pretty persuasive fellow. Especially when you're tired."

"Ha. Ha. Yes, I'm stubborn. But you still love me."

That he did. More than she knew.

The Kidnapping of Cody Moss

Chapter Thirty-One

As promised, Zach woke her at eleven and they drove to the lab. The techs weren't ecstatic to see them waiting at the door, but Annalise hoped they understood the urgency of the situation and forgave her.

Zach whispered to one of the guys at a microscope.

They looked at her, hovering in the doorway, in unison. She raised a hand and finger-waved. What had Zach said? Was her hair a disaster? She touched a hand to the ponytail.

Zach returned to her side. "You look great. It's not that. I was just telling Scott who you are and why this is so important."

"And?"

"He totally understands. He is printing results now."

She caught Scott's eye on his next retreat from the microscope and smiled, passing I'm-sorry-to-rush-you vibes along with it. When had she ever thought about being a bother? These professionals were doing their jobs, and they fully understood why a kidnapping took priority. Dave's criticisms had really hit home, hadn't they? She shook her shoulders to release some of the tension. She was being ridiculous.

And Zach could read her mind. He smiled like a Cheshire cat.

She swatted his arm. "Stop it. Or I'll have to put aluminum foil on my head."

He burst out laughing. "I hadn't thought about that particular nightmare in years."

"That's because the aliens made you forget it all when you got back to Earth."

"Oh, right. I forgot."

She chuckled briefly but grew serious as Scott approached.

"Here you go. Most likely a man's boot, size thirteen. A bit of an unusual wear pattern, and if you have the boot to compare, we might be able to make a definitive match." He handed her a thick binder labeled Brands of Shoes, Treads, and Prints. "This is the master copy. Don't lose it or spill anything on it. Okay?"

"Thanks."

"There is an empty conference room next door. And here is the photocopied image. I hope you find a match."

She nodded. It was a long shot, but maybe God was already working in the details today. And she did like puzzles.

Zach held the door for her to the conference room. "I'll be right back. Gonna go check with Kirk and see if he's heard anything from anyone at TBI."

"Okay. I'll be here. With this." She held up the thick binder and sighed. *Lord, a little luck, please?*

She flipped through pages and pages of different boots, each labeled by the manufacturer and referencing an index with local sellers. Many of the prints looked the same except for very subtle changes in the angle of a tread. It could take all day to compare each and every one.

Maybe she needed to start backward. Jimmy Vern lived between Gatlinburg and Pigeon Forge. She did a quick Google search on her phone for shoe stores nearby and moaned when it returned over fifty results.

She pressed her eyes closed and leaned back into the office chair. *All right, Annalise. If you were Jimmy Vern, where would you shop?* Wal-Mart. Where most Southern Americans bought most of their items. She flipped to the index at the back and found the Wal-Mart heading. Upon quick perusal, it seemed most of the locations sold pretty much the same stock. Most likely, he'd go to the one closest to home, the Pigeon Forge location.

With the photo in one hand, she compared it carefully to each of the dozen or so known prints from Wal-Mart's Brahma, Ozark Trail, and Herman boot lines. There! Though she only had about half a print, there was no doubt she'd found the match. She whipped out her phone and texted Zach. "I've got it. Come back!"

He burst into the room with a big grin a minute later. "You found it?"

"Yep. Come on. We're going to Wal-Mart."

"Okay…"

"Brahma boots. Wal-Mart." She grinned. "I'll buy you a snack."

"Deal."

She returned the album to the lab and hugged Scott.

His jaw dropped, and he didn't raise his arms to hug her back.

It wasn't like her at all to be so impulsive. But oh, well. Her excitement had spilled over. It was the first potential chance of pinning this on Jimmy Vern, and getting him to disclose Cody's location, they'd had in days.

"So, how about that snack you promised me?" Zach nudged Annalise and smiled.

She rolled her eyes. "Yeah, yeah. Give me a few more minutes."

He crossed his arms and leaned against the tall shelving behind him. It was good to see her spirits higher and a smile tugging at her lips when he teased.

"Ah. Got it." She pulled a box from the shelf and opened it. "Look." She compared the bottom of the boot to the printout Scott had given them.

"Looks identical. Good job."

"Thanks." She put the lid on the box and headed for the checkout. "Let's get back."

"Um, snacks are that way." He pointed toward the grocery section of the store.

"Meet you at the checkout. Twenty-dollar limit. Okay, bottomless pit?"

"Twenty bucks!" He shouted at her disappearing-between-the-clothes-racks-back.

She raised a hand and half-waved.

He chuckled. This was the woman he knew. Playful yet intelligent. Focused and smart. She would be okay. Eventually. Once they found Cody and she had time to process Dave's infidelity, she would bounce back and be stronger than ever. *Right, Lord?*

Zach grabbed chips and cheese dip, beef jerky, and sodas. At the last minute, he threw in some grapes for Annalise and wound his way to the front of the store. He caught sight of Annalise at checkout one and stopped in his tracks.

This was his Annalise. His best friend for more than two decades. But something seemed so different. He'd never looked at her in any way other than through the lens of friendship. Why, then, did her gorgeous blonde hair, the self-confident tilt of her chin, and her hazel eyes flashing his direction make his heart skip right now? He shook his head.

She was a damsel in distress. That was it. His hero complex kicking in and making him feel things that weren't real or appropriate.

After all, she was a married woman, and he would never, ever dream of interfering in someone's vows. *Lord, forgive me for these thoughts. Make them go away and let me be the friend—strictly platonic friend—that she needs right now.*

Annalise paid for his snacks, with one more eye roll and grin for good measure, and the boots. Back in the truck, she turned to him. "Can you call Kirk? I have a question."

"Sure." He pressed speed dial number three and waited. "Hey, man. I'm going to put you on speaker phone with Annalise."

"Hey, Kirk. Do you know if Jimmy Vern's financial records are still being watched?"

Zach's smile spread. Annalise was back in investigator mode. And she was so good at it, her mind thinking of details to cover all bases and bring the bad guys to justice.

"I don't believe so. He is on probation from the moonshine charges, but as far as I know, no open or active investigation is running against him."

Annalise put the truck in drive as she spoke. "We need a way to link these boots to his purchases. If we can positively identify him purchasing this same type, I have no doubt we could get a warrant."

"You're absolutely right, Baker." Kirk paused. "Meet me at Cracker Barrel in twenty minutes.

Someone owes me a favor, and it may be time to call it in."

"Great. Thanks. We are so close, guys, I can feel it."

Zach sure hoped so. He wanted this win for Annalise. She desperately needed one right now.

Zach held the door for her. She smiled as she entered the lobby and glanced over the knick-knacks for sale. "Is this your guys' new office?"

"Hardy har. Very funny."

"What? It's perfect for you. A steady supply of delicious food. A country theme that should make you country boys feel right at home. Plus no clean up."

Zach scratched his chin. "You have a point."

Annalise chuckled. "Is Kirk here yet?"

"You know, I may just talk to him about this brilliant observation of yours. They haven't finished adding the new headquarters wing for SMIF onto City Hall yet. This could be the perfect solution."

"Focus, Zach. Do you see Kirk?"

"What? Oh, yeah. He's at our table, in the corner near the fireplace." He pointed. "It is the best seat in the house, with the sound, smell, and warmth of the fire. Plus the waitress working that section is cute."

Oh, brother. She punched him in the shoulder. "You're a mess."

"Hot mess. You forgot the word hot."

It felt so good to laugh. Zach had always been able to do that. Make her laugh when she felt like crying. Make her smile when she felt like screaming. He was a good balance for her. She thought Dave was too, but that was before…She didn't want to finish the thought. It was the first time in the last two hours worries about Dave had crept in. Ugh. Not now, heart. Not yet. We are not ready to process it all yet.

They joined Kirk at the table. Zach pulled out a menu, but Annalise couldn't think about eating. "What did you find out?"

Kirk slid her a stack of papers. "Bank statements for the last year."

"How did you—"

He held up one finger and shook his head. "Ah, ah, ah. I can't talk about it."

"Thank you."

"We're all on the same team."

Not technically. She hadn't accepted the job offer. She could now, though, couldn't she? Dave wouldn't have a say in it. Unless they decided to go to marriage counseling and try to save…Could she even forgive him for having an affair, if he would agree to go see a therapist? The waitress interrupted her musing.

"What can I get you folks?"

The guys ordered big meals.

"Grilled chicken salad for me and some highlighters."

The waitress stopped writing. "Excuse me?"

"Highlighters. Do you have any we could borrow?"

"Um, yeah, maybe. Let me check in the kitchen."

"Working lunch, eh?" Zach lifted his eyebrow.

"We don't have any time to waste." She split the large stack of papers into thirds and handed Kirk and Zach each a part. "We are looking for Wal-Mart purchases."

The waitress returned with their drinks, a basket of cornbread and biscuits, and three yellow markers. "These work?"

"Yes, thank you." Annalise took them. "Okay, guys, highlight any lines of sales at Wal-Mart, and just to be safe, any shoe stores you see as well."

Kirk took a marker. "You should know, these records will probably be inadmissible in court."

She figured as much. Called-in favors usually didn't play by the rules. Annalise shrugged. "It's okay. When we find Cody, Jimmy Vern will drive the nails into his own coffin. We will have enough to take him down, without these bank records."

At first, whenever one of them found a Wal-Mart purchase, they called out to the others, but as their meals were consumed and their highlighters drained on more than fifty different transactions, the table grew quiet.

Zach patted her hand. "How do you eat an elephant?"

She smiled weakly. "One bite at a time."

"Right. Kirk, can you work on the paperwork? We will head over to the store now and wait for your word."

Kirk cleared his throat. "No paperwork. I can't submit the bank records as justification." He cracked a large grin. "You're going to have to use your charm, Special Agent Leebow."

Zach flashed his biggest smile at the woman behind the help desk. "We need to speak to the manager, please."

The clerk frowned but lifted the receiver and paged Honey Lee to the front.

A middle-aged woman with crow's feet and a smile greeted them. "How may I help you, officers?"

"We were hoping we could ask you for a favor."

"Oh?"

"We are looking for a missing teenager, and we believe his kidnapper shopped here. If we can get him on video purchasing a pair of boots—" Zach pointed to the ones Annalise lifted "—we can get the warrant we need to search his property."

Honey frowned. "I'm sorry. It's corporate's policy not to release any video recordings without the proper paperwork."

Zach was afraid she might say that. "We would really appreciate it. And it just might save the boy's life."

She sighed. "I want to help. I really do, but I could lose my job."

Zach glanced at Annalise, who wore a disappointed scowl. "Is there anything I can do or say to change your mind?"

"I might be able to…no. No, I really can't. I'm so sorry."

"We understand," Annalise said.

"Thanks anyway." Zach flashed an "I'm sorry" half-grin to Annalise.

Honey walked away, and Annalise leaned in. "Ready to do it my way now?"

There wasn't anything left to do but give her plan a try. At this point, what could they lose?

Chapter Thirty-Two

Where was he? Cody's head throbbed. His ears were full and sounds were muffled. What was happening?

"I thought you was dead, boy."

He startled at the sound of Jimmy Vern's voice nearby. He peeled his eyes open and blinked. Treetops? Hard to tell against the backdrop of the night sky, but the ground beneath him wasn't the dirt floor of the cellar. He gripped handfuls of leaves. For the first time in days, his heart grew fuller. This was his chance at escape!

If he could move.

Jimmy Vern had drugged him again, hadn't he? His limbs were too heavy, like tree trunks instead of arms and legs. He struggled to reach a sitting position. Jimmy Vern's wet boot crushed his chest and pressed him back to the earth.

"You're too drunk to get up and run. Don't try."

Drunk? He'd only had one big sip out of that awful jug. "Wh—what are you doing with me?"

"Hiding your body."

What? Hiding his…what? How could he…Cody had to have heard him wrong.

"This woulda been much easier if you just died. You didn't have a pulse. How are you alive?"

He hadn't had a pulse? Nothing Jimmy Vern said made any sense. Clearly he was alive, with a pulse and a somewhat intact brain.

The sound of rushing water reached him.

Jimmy Vern slid his hands under Cody's shoulders and dragged him, muttering more to himself than to Cody. "I drugged you and gave you liquor. You should be dead."

His mind and heart screamed, but no part of his body would cooperate. This couldn't be happening. He flailed his arms, but it may as well have been a baby reaching for a mobile over his crib as much good as it did him. He had given up, had resigned to death. Now that it seemed inevitable, he realized with all his being that he didn't want to die. *Lord, I need You!*

Pain lanced the base of his skull, and then he was falling. Down and down through empty space. He tried to scream, but nothing would come out.

He splashed into cold, black water and sank. His fingertips tingled with the sudden chill. And suddenly his heart sprang into action, pounding in his ears. He fought his way upward and gasped, his pulse pounding in his throat. The current was too strong, his head spinning too fast. There was no way to fight the downward pull.

When the first rays of rosy dawn pierced the sky, Annalise was waiting at the end of Jimmy Vern's driveway. Zach and Kirk hadn't spoken much since she'd given them both full details of her ideas, but they must have agreed. They were here, after all.

Without a warrant, they'd agreed that stealth was better than brawn, at least.

Annalise snapped her helmet in place, tightened the Velcro over her shoulders, and flipped the gun safety off. "Ready?"

The men nodded in unison.

She turned and drew a deep breath, comforted by the muted crunch of their feet on gravel following close at her heels. This was it. The chance she'd waited for. With the money as bait, though they lacked firm evidence of Jimmy Vern's guilt, they would be able to get him to talk. To trade Cody to them. And then they'd take Jimmy Vern down.

It sounded so good in her head, but each step closer nailed more worries into her mind. Zach had been right to be skeptical. She stopped in her tracks.

"See something?" Zach hissed in her ear.

She shook her head.

"It's a good plan, Annalise."

It was the only one they had.

"Let's get in there. Cody's counting on you."

Kirk squeezed her shoulder. "Trust your instincts."

They hadn't gotten her very far lately. But Zach was right, Cody needed them. She resumed her slow approach.

A single light shined from the cabin windows. Jimmy Vern's rusty truck sat in the driveway. Good. He was home.

Annalise took cover behind the truck, motioning for Zach and Kirk to slide around each side of the house. She counted to 120 and then yelled, "Jimmy Vern Buchanan. We have your money."

Where were the dogs? And why didn't they come out barking like the world was ending?

There was no noise within the cabin, but a shadow passed across the window.

"Jimmy Vern! Come on out. We need to talk."

The front window shattered in an explosion of popping glass, immediately followed by the roar of a shotgun blast. Pellets thunked into the truck. The dogs broke into a loud ruckus from somewhere inside.

Annalise ducked. Her ear piece crackled to life with Zach's worried voice. "You okay?"

"Yes, stand down. Hold your positions, guys. Watch for the dogs, if he lets them loose."

She cupped her hand around her mouth and tried once more. "If you shoot me, you'll never find your ten grand!"

Another shot blasted the air.

She counted slowly to sixty, drawing deep breaths. This was going to work, right? "Jimmy Vern! Last chance!"

The creak of the front door sounded almost as loud as the gunshots. Jimmy Vern stepped onto the porch. "You found my stolen money?"

"Yes." She risked standing up. Though he held the gun across his arm, he wasn't aiming at anything in particular. That was a move in the right direction. The door behind him jiggled. The dogs barked again.

"I wanna see it."

"It's not with me. You know I'm smarter than that. But I can get it, if you give me Cody."

"I don't know nothing about that missing boy." Jimmy Vern's hand drew closer to the doorknob.

She bit her tongue. Hard. And tasted copper. "We know you're involved. It was your man murdered at that campsite. The boys stole your money from there."

"I didn't know the money was missing until you showed me that photo of Buster."

"Why did Buster have ten thousand dollars of your money in the middle of the woods?"

"Was taking it to the bank for me."

Oh, sure. That was logical. "Don't open that door, Jimmy Vern. We will shoot them."

Red colored his face, but he dropped his hand.

She caught movement out of the corner of her eye. Zach and Kirk were sneaking closer along the sides of the house. "Who killed Buster, Jimmy Vern?"

He shrugged.

"Whose still was that?"

Another shrug.

"Have it your way. Move in."

Jimmy Vern's eyes widened. He spun and opened the door. "Get 'em, boys."

The dogs barreled out, baring their teeth, back fur raised into an arch, and barking.

Annalise jumped onto the hood of the truck.

The Rottweiler snapped at her left heel and planted his paws on the grill. The mutt ran in wild circles around the truck.

Zach and Kirk waited for her command, guns aimed at Jimmy Vern.

She scrambled to the windshield and aimed for the massive mouth. "One, two. Don't test me…" She squeezed the trigger.

"Fine, fine." Jimmy Vern whistled.

Instantly, the dogs retreated under the porch.

She blew out a heavy breath. "We are taking you in for questioning, Jimmy Vern. I'm sure we can find something to charge you with."

Zach and Kirk moved in simultaneously. They cuffed Jimmy Vern, and Kirk held him in the corner of the porch.

"You hear that?" Zach cocked his head.

All Annalise could hear was the pounding of her heart.

Kirk grinned. "Sure do."

What were they talking about?

"Sounds like someone screaming back there toward the barn, doesn't it, Jimmy Vern?" Zach smiled.

"That's my mule, and you know it."

Ah. The perfect excuse to search the premises. "No, I think I hear it too now."

"Come on, Annalise. Kirk, you got him?"

Kirk nodded.

Annalise followed Zach toward the barn with her stomach vying with her heart for top position in her throat. This could be it. Cody could be on the other side of those doors somewhere.

Zach slid the door open. "Cody! Cody!"

A horse whinnied, but no human voice responded.

"Search everywhere, okay? Look for hidden doors and rooms."

"Yes, ma'am." Zach grinned. "I like when you take charge, Lise. This job looks good on you."

She blushed and shook her head. "I didn't say yes. Let's focus on finding him."

They split up. Annalise climbed the stairs to the loft and searched through the innumerable bales of hay. Jimmy Vern had apparently told the truth about that part, at least.

What if there was a tunnel into a hay-room of some sort, hiding in the middle of the giant stack? She and her brother had done that in their grandparents' barn as children. "Cody! If you can hear me, make some noise."

If Jimmy Vern kept his prisoner drugged, Cody wouldn't be able to make any noise. She holstered her gun and slid some of the bales at the edges around. There didn't seem to be any gaps anywhere.

Zach's steps clumped behind her into the loft. "Find anything?"

"No. Was checking to make sure there wasn't some tunnel or hidden area under this."

"I'll help."

Before she could argue, Zach leaped onto the nearest bale and climbed the stack like a mountain goat. "Be careful!"

"Always." He stopped at the top, a good fifteen feet higher than her, and looked back. "I don't see anything that would lead me to believe there is anything hidden underneath. Except rats and snakes, maybe."

Her heart sank. If Cody wasn't here—if there wasn't some hidden, tucked-away niche they would miraculously find—then where was he? She'd been so sure the barn would house not only a moonshine still but her missing child too.

"I need to show you something downstairs."

She followed him to the two last stalls on the right and peeked in. A mule and a horse. "What do you know about that?"

"Did you collect manure samples from the moonshine still site?"

Annalise grinned. "Sure did."

"Knew I could count on you to cover all the bases." He collected a manure sample from each equine inside two latex gloves. "Let's rush this to the lab."

"If they match, we have enough evidence to search the house."

"And arrest Jimmy Vern."

Chapter Thirty-Three

"It's a match!" Zach grabbed Annalise and swung her around, hugging her tight.

She exhaled and laid her head on his shoulder. "I knew it was him. I just knew it. Let's find Cody."

The dogs growled at them from the pen where they'd insisted Jimmy Vern lock them. He had unwillingly accompanied Kirk on his rush into town with the samples. His destination at the end of the day largely depended on what he and Annalise found.

Annalise swung the front door in and disappeared.

Good. "I'll check the cellar," he shouted after her. If Cody was down there, dead already, he wanted to find him first and break the news gently to Annalise.

The cellar door had been padlocked shut. Suspicious. He found a pickax nearby and broke it open with a few heavy strikes. He tugged hard and lifted the heavy wood panel open. A horrible odor met his nose, and his hopes fell even further. *Oh, Lord, please. Not this ending. Not this way.*

His steps grew heavier as he descended, and the stench grew stronger. He shined his flashlight into the corners, stopping on the farthest one. What was that? It certainly didn't seem large enough to be a human body.

He covered his nose with his shirt and eased into the area. Someone had been here and been very, very sick. A dead rat lay at the edge of the nauseating pile. He backed away, and he searched the rest of the area. There was nothing here and nowhere to hide.

Drawing a deep breath of fresh air at the top of the steps, he sighed. He hadn't found Cody, but he hadn't found a body either. And that was a positive. "Annalise!" he called as he entered the cabin.

"In here!"

He followed the sound of her voice to the room on the right. A tiny kitchen boasted a messy table with one chair and rows and rows of empty Mason jars. *Oh, gee, wonder what those were for.* "Find something?"

"Maybe." She lifted a credit card from the trash bin.

"Brian Moss. Think Cody had this?"

"I'd say it's a good possibility."

"I need to show you something too."

Her face paled. "What is it? Is it…is he dead?"

He shook his head. "I think he was here though." He led her to the stairs and stopped her. "You may want to cover your mouth and nose."

Her eyes grew wide. She nodded.

When he reached the bottom, he stopped and let Annalise explore and see for herself. His heart ached for her as she made her way slowly around the space.

When she reached the corner, she sank to her heels and froze.

What was she thinking? For once he didn't know.

"He was here, Zach."

"I think so too."

"No, I mean he was here. Come look."

In the opposite corner from the dead rat, low on the wall, shined shallow hash marks. Five of them. "That means—"

"He was here yesterday." Annalise turned to him with tear-filled eyes.

So where was he now? Were they only a day late? Only a few hours too late to save the boy? *Why, Lord?*

He pulled Annalise into his arms. He longed to offer comforting words, but he couldn't find a single one. She'd poured her heart into finding Cody, and to come here and find out she'd missed her window by only a few hours? It was too cruel. *Why, Lord?*

Annalise pulled away, her teeth gritted and her eyes dark. "Take me to Jimmy Vern. Now."

"Annal—"

"I will bring Cody's body home for his mother. She deserves to give him a proper burial."

He swallowed the lump in his throat. "Okay, Annalise. Okay."

Annalise held the tears in only by focusing on the intense anger roiling in her chest.

"We're on our way, Kirk," Zach said from the passenger seat. "Yeah…we need to speak to Jimmy Vern…yeah, alone." He ended the call. "Kirk agreed."

"Did you tell him…everything?"

"Yes. The forensics team is on their way to the cabin now."

"Good." They could at least collect enough evidence to seal Jimmy Vern's case. "Dogs?"

"They're going to try "

Maybe Jimmy Vern just moved Cody since he felt their team closing in. "Good. Maybe they'll—"

"Cadaver dogs, Annalise."

Blood rushed to her head. Cadaver dogs. Of course. She sandwiched her head between her knees and took deep breaths. "I really thought we would find him."

Zach rubbed her back with his free hand. "I know you did. I'm so sorry, Annalise."

"You didn't think…you knew, didn't you?"

"I didn't know anything." He sighed. "And neither do you yet. Not for sure."

"There's no point, Zach. It's time to face reality. Cody's dead. I will have to consider it a win, now, putting that monster behind bars and finding Cody's remains."

He grimaced but remained silent.

What could he say?

In Memphis, after her first few years of death and brutality, she had gone somewhat numb. And she'd stayed that way, hadn't she? Was this what Dave had been talking about when he said she was too independent? Too self-sufficient? When really it was too scarred?

Scarred. Did she think of herself as broken? Jaded?

The thoughts kept her breath just out of reach.

Zach pulled the truck onto the shoulder. Semis whizzed by and shook the truck. He hopped out and ran around to her side, yanking the door open. "Look at me."

Had he really just risked being smattered on the side of the road for her? "That was dumb, Zach."

"Look at me."

She turned her head to face him.

"Dave was wrong. Okay? Dead wrong." He wrinkled his brow. "Sorry. Poor choice of words. The point is, you are amazing."

She shook her head. No, she was selfish and self-absorbed to the point her husband had sought attention in someone else's arms.

"You deserve better. Someone who will cherish you and treat you like the wonderful person you are."

"I failed. Dave and Cody and Celine."

"And yourself."

"Uh-huh."

"And me."

"Uh-huh." Wait. "How did I fail you?"

"By being so hard on yourself. This isn't you, and you know it. Get Dave out of your head. He is a fool." He tugged her chin up, reminding her to look him in the eye. "God can work good from all things, even if it feels like the world is ending. You just have to keep believing and keep going."

"I can't."

He tilted his head.

"Okay, fine. I don't want to."

He arched his eyebrow.

She growled. "Fine. You win. Pity party over."

"There's my girl."

His girl? Why did it suddenly sound so different from all the other times he'd said it? She swallowed the rest of her crazy emotions. "Thanks. Let's go get him."

He patted her knees and kissed her forehead. "Good."

They met Kirk at the gas station off the Midland exit.

Annalise reached for the door handle, but Zach grabbed her arm.

"Take a deep breath."

"I'm good." Resolution settled a calming weight over her mind and heart. Until this really was over, she would hold it together.

Kirk pulled Jimmy Vern from the passenger rear of his car.

Still in handcuffs, Jimmy Vern's red face dripped with sweat. "You can't keep me like this!" He spat into the leaves. "I will press charges."

She stopped toe-to-toe and stared deep into his eyes. Ten seconds, twenty, thirty.

His mouth clamped tight, and he took a step back.

"I know Cody was there." She laid her hands on his shoulders. "And you will tell me—look at me, Jimmy Vern Buchanan—"

He brought his wide eyes back to hers.

"Where his body is, so I can take him home to his momma."

"Or what?"

She leaned in, so close she could see the closed-up piercing in his earlobe. "I will put your body somewhere no one, and I mean no one, will find you. After I starve you for five days like you did him."

"I didn't starve—" Jimmy Vern clamped his mouth shut.

"Arrest him, Kirk. That's as good as a confession for me." Annalise moved quickly enough that Jimmy Vern flinched. She spun him back toward the truck and slammed the door on his protests. He made her physically ill. "Get him out of here. I can't look at him a minute longer."

Kirk stared at her, open mouthed. He swallowed and regained his composure. "I'll get it out of him before we get to the jail, Annalise. Get back out there and see if you can find the boy's—" He winced. "Get back up there."

"Yes, sir."

Zach smiled at her. "I'm proud of you."

For what? She hadn't gotten any real, helpful answers.

"For not taking his sorry hind end out right now."

She chuckled. "I wanted to."

"But you acted responsibly. Like the upstanding officer and child of God you are. That's the difference between him and you."

He was right. And it did feel good to know the truth. Jimmy Vern was guilty of kidnapping, moonshine making, and now, probably, double murder. He would never see the light of day again, if she had anything to say about it.

They pulled into the driveway, now backed up with emergency personnel vehicles almost to the road.

She twisted her hands in her lap. "Think they found anything yet?" Even though it seemed the odds were in the negative, the thought they would find him alive crept back in. *Wouldn't that be a wonderful miracle, Lord?*

"They would have called."

"Yeah."

"Ready?"

"Give me a minute."

He stepped out.

She bowed her head. *I need You, Lord. I'm about to give up. You know my heart. You know how badly we all want to find Cody and bring him home. One way or another.*

I'm here. I've always been here, child.

Tears popped into her eyes. *I need strength.*

You need to trust.

It hurts too much, God. I trusted Dave, and he betrayed me.

I have a plan. In all of it.

She raised her eyes to the mountains covered in reds, yellows, and golds. A strong wind kicked up, rustling their brilliant fringes together and rushing toward the valley. God was here. In the middle of all this pain. In the middle of her heart, and in the middle of the sorrow. No matter what happened, He could bring good, maybe even joy again someday. If she chose to focus on Him, and not the problem, He would bring a solution.

The freedom she felt in that revelation washed over her like the cool wind. It lifted her out of the truck and up the driveway. As she stood, with her hands planted on her hips, and surveyed Jimmy Vern's property, Zach's phone rang.

"Kirk, what have you found out?"

Annalise held her breath. This was it. The moment when the path would lead to a funeral or a celebration. Which would it be?

"Okay. Thanks." Zach hung the phone up and turned to her. "Kirk got Jimmy Vern to tell him where he took Cody."

She raised her eyebrows.

"Jimmy Vern said the boy wasn't dead when he left him."

Her mind and heart and soul leapt for joy, almost as if she could physically feel them rising upward within her. "Where?"

"Come on." He grabbed her hand and pulled her back to his truck, then kicking it into 4-wheel drive, slung around the parked vehicles, raced past the cabin, and headed for the far end of the valley.

Lord, please, repeated a mantra in her mind as the wind whipped her face through the open window.

Chapter Thirty-Four

Zach pulled to a grassy bald and slammed the truck in park. They leapt out together and ran to the area where the weeds had been pressed down by tires recently, still carrying the imprint of Jimmy Vern's tread.

The cliff in front of them ended in a too-full creek forty feet below. Annalise gasped. "Did he really throw him from here?" How could someone do that? She'd asked that question so many times over the years. She'd never understand how human beings could be so cruel to one another.

Zach nodded.

They studied the shoreline below, and her heart stopped rejoicing. Was there any way he could have survived that?

"Not likely, Annalise."

There Zach was, reading her mind again. "We need to get down there."

"Follow me."

Zach wound his way through the forest next to the field and finally found a little-used path down the bluff. A game trail, maybe. It sloped to meet a wider, slower section of the creek.

Annalise stopped to check the banks from their still-higher perch. The air whooshed from her lungs. "Zach, look!" She pointed at a dark-clad lump hidden under the edge of a rhododendron. Was that really him?

Her heart pounded in rhythm to her running steps. She knelt next to him and paused. *Lord, help me.* With a trembling hand, she reached to feel his back. Too cool. Too still.

Zach squatted next to her.

"I can't reach his neck."

"We shouldn't move him if—"

"I can't just narrowly miss again." She pressed him with a pleading gaze and lowered her voice. "I have to know for sure."

He pressed his lips together but nodded.

"Help me?"

Zach pushed through the thick branches and held them back while she lifted Cody's limp body.

She laid him gently in a patch of sunshine. She pressed two fingers to his neck and held her breath. *Lord, please. Please. Please.*

A dull thump bounced against her fingers. Several seconds later, another.

"He's alive!"

"I don't believe it."

Annalise couldn't take her eyes off Cody's thin, pale face, but from somewhere behind her, she heard Zach dial and request a helicopter.

"They'll be here in ten minutes, but they have to land up top."

If Cody could survive Jimmy Vern for five days and being thrown into a creek, surely carrying him wouldn't push him over the edge.

"Zach?"

He nodded and scooped Cody into his arms.

She covered him with her sweater. "I'll lead the way." Her feet floated her up the narrow path. By the time they got there, the helicopter's blades cut the air overhead. Annalise helped guide them to the ground.

Once the doors slid open, the medics took charge and loaded Cody in a matter of seconds. She didn't have time to breathe until they were zipping away over the treetops. *Lord, thank you!* She turned and buried her head in Zach's chest.

He wrapped his arms around her.

The sobs she'd needed to release for days broke free. All the things Dave had said and done, all the fears for Cody and his family, all the sense of inadequacy and worry and disappointment came out in her salty tears. So much tension ebbed out of her body, a few minutes later she wanted to curl into the grass and sleep for a month.

Zach pulled back and smiled.

She turned her face and swiped at her cheeks. "I'm a mess. Been a long time since I ugly-cried."

He chuckled. "Even when you 'ugly cry,' Annalise, you're beautiful. Come on, let's get to the hospital."

She nodded. "Oh! I have to call Celine. Now."

"I am so proud of you for not giving up. You knew in your heart of hearts he was going to make it."

"He still may not." It was a miracle to have found him at all. Maybe it would be a two-part miracle. *Lord?*

Zach had heard of women who glowed when they got pregnant and had babies. Annalise glowed when she found someone else's child. And he only loved her all the more for it.

They drove in silence to LeConte Medical Center. By the time they located Cody, he'd been taken into the ICU Trauma bay and could have no visitors.

Annalise's shoulders drooped.

"Come on, let's go wait for Celine. She'll need a friendly face."

He led her to a seat in the quiet room and answered the call breaking the stillness. "Kirk, get anything out of him?"

"Full confession."

No way. "Really?" It was the second time in the last hour he'd been astonished at the outcome of this case.

"About everything."

"How'd you do it?"

"Threatened his dogs."

"You've got to be kidding."

"Dead serious. He told me everything. From how they ran supplies in from both sides of the mountain, Cataloochee and Pigeon Forge, by horseback. Made the moonshine and brought it down on foot with hikers. They used the backcountry trails and sites."

That explained the broken glass at the campsite. "Why did he kill Buster?"

"He claims Buster threatened to take more than his fair cut. They got in a huge fight. Jimmy Vern shot him, and while he was dumping the body the kids happened to come along. Jimmy Vern saw them running and then found Cody's dad's credit card and tracked them down."

"Wow."

"I know. Ten thousand dollars is highly motivating though."

"For anyone."

"True. When he found out about Cody, he grabbed him, locked him in the cellar, and tried to get him to tell where the money was. When that didn't work, he attacked Celine and torched Paul's house."

"Is there anything that man won't do?"

Annalise was boring him through with her questioning gaze.

He held up a finger and whispered, "Hang on."

"He figured we were closing in, and the boy got ill off some bad chicken he fed him, so he tried to tie up that loose end too."

"Lucky for us, that particular one didn't work."

"How is Cody?"

"We don't really know anything right now."

"I'm processing Jimmy Vern now. Oh, and the hit on Wilson too."

"How did he manage that one?"

"He met some interesting people when he was in jail the first time. As dumb as the man looks, he has a good head for business under there."

"Clever, conniving man."

"You've got that right. Okay, call me if you hear something about Cody."

"I will. Thanks, Kirk."

"This time I can say, my pleasure, and mean it. Oh, hey, tell Annalise I'm still waiting for her yes."

Zach chuckled as he hung up. He told Annalise everything.

Her smile grew wider and wider.

"He says you need to say yes."

She bit her cheek.

"What's stopping you?" Dave either would agree to work things out and support her, or he would show his true colors and leave. Annalise passing up the offer would only hurt her. *Let her say yes, Lord. Show her it's okay.*

A slow smile broke over her face. "Nothing. I'm in."

He hugged her. "I knew you'd say yes."

She slapped his shoulder. "You did, huh? I didn't even know until right now. But bringing Cody home for his mother feels amazing."

He wrinkled his brow. "They won't all end like this."

"I know. I want to be there for the ones that do, though."

They spun at a commotion in the outer lobby. Spotting them, Celine stepped through the doors, breathless. "Have you seen him yet?"

Annalise put her hand on her shoulder. "No." Celine fell into her arms, and Annalise hugged her close.

"Was he…is he…"

Annalise led Celine to the nearest chair. "He was unconscious when I found him. Barely had a pulse, and breathing was almost nonexistent."

Celine choked on a sob.

"But he was alive. That's the important part." Annalise smiled. "We never know how many miracles God has planned for him."

"Thank you for saying that." She wiped her tears with a tissue.

"How are you feeling?"

"Much better. They discharged me home with concussion precautions. I probably shouldn't have driven here, but I couldn't wait."

Zach grinned. "I think under the circumstances, any officer who happened to pull you over would have given you a police escort straight here and held your hand—you know the one not in a cast—while you found your son."

Celine chuckled. "Thanks, Officer Leebow. Brian is on his way back in too."

Annalise smiled and patted her hand. "We have good news, Ms. Moss."

Her gaze snapped up to meet theirs. "Besides finding my son, you mean?"

"The man who orchestrated all of this—kidnapped Cody, attacked you—all of it, is behind bars and will be staying there for a very, very long time."

Celine melted against Annalise's side with another round of tears.

A nurse burst through the doors, wearing a broad smile. "Family of Cody Moss?"

The three of them rose to their feet as one unit. "Yes."

"He's awake."

Dear Readers,

I hope you have enjoyed book number one in my new Smoky Mountain Suspense series. It was, at times, a challenging one to write, but in the end what truly matters is that I effectively communicate the great love God has for you. He is always able to work good from the things we sometimes see as the worst possible outcome. His answers may not always be miracles, or even line up with what we ask, but ultimately He wants what's best for you.

Check out book number two, *The Vanishing of Olivia Beck*, which is available for preorder on Amazon now. Coming April 2020!

She is looking forward to a new beginning in a new town...

Until an old case heats up again and a familiar face brings the past back to life. Recently recruited Special Agents Annalise Baker and Zachary Leebow are called upon to investigate major crimes in the Great Smoky Mountains. Now, with a missing woman that seems a bit too familiar and a former arrestee out for vengeance, these best friends are not only tasked with solving a puzzling disappearance...

...but running for their own lives.

Pssst.. Just a quick reminder, if you haven't already, please join my newsletter. I'd love to have you! Sign up now and get my free eBook novella, *Of Walls*, delivered right to your inbox. Plus get the inside scoop on all of my new releases and giveaways and receive monthly newsletters where we can connect, get to know each other, and pray for one another. Here is the link (or click on the image below): http://eepurl.com/cfqP5H

Would you like a FREE book? For being part of my News Friends, you can receive a free ebook copy of my women's fiction novella, Of Walls.

Acknowledgments

Thank you, Athena Brown, for naming the villain in this book. It was so fun asking readers to help me come up with a name, and I got so many great suggestions! Jimmy Vern Buchanan just seemed to fit, though.

I could not have gotten this far—or even continued writing at all—without the help and support of my family. I'm always so afraid I will forget someone, but I will try. Special thanks to:

Chelsea, my kids' favorite non-grandparent babysitter, my confidant, my friend. I am so thankful for you.

Aunt Sue, you have bought multiple copies of each of my books and never hesitated to help me out when my world turned upside down this last year. From the bottom of my heart, thank you.

Becky (number one), you encourage me and keep me going when I worry I will never succeed. You read everything I write and never hesitate to give me honest advice. You've been my professional artist consultor and therapist and best friend all at the same time. I only wish Texas was in Tennessee.

Becky (number two), you have listened to my tears so many times this past year and you have talked all things books with me when others' eyes glaze over. I am so blessed to call you friend.

Mom and Dad, you have rearranged your schedules more times than I can count to watch my crazy crew, have supported and listened and provided for and loved me from day one. God couldn't have picked better parents for me.

Caleb and Leia, you've never hesitated to send me praise and encouragement when I've needed it, and I am so thankful. Plus, bro, you put up with my crazy clan of cats for the night just so I wouldn't be alone…thanks, again.

Aunt Vicki, you, too, have bought all my books and shared them with your family. You always have a smile and a hug for me. Thank you.

Valerie, you've listened, given advice, and prayed with me. You've made me laugh and encouraged me.

Aunt Jeanne, you've been so encouraging and made me feel so special for being an author. Thank you for that and for helping support the kids and me when we needed it this year.

Brett and Kate—reasons. Thank you, truly.

Abby, Emma, Mayci, Korrie, and Cole, thank you for being the ones who call me Mommy. I know you had no choice or say in the matter, but it is an honor nonetheless. I am beyond blessed to be your mother. Thank you for letting me write, for watching over each other and sticking together, and, most of all, letting me love you.

All of my family is amazing. I could never express how very thankful I am to be placed exactly as I am in this world. I can't repay you for all you've done. I love each and every one of you!

Most of all, I thank God. He has been my closest friend, my biggest encourager, and my guide, in life and in writing. Without Him none of this would be possible.

I am one blessed girl!

About the Author

Sara is a multi-published, award-winning author and homeschooling mother of five who writes surrounded by the beauty of East Tennessee. She earned her bachelor's degree in Animal Science from the University of Tennessee and is a member of American Christian Fiction Writers. She is the author of the Love, Hope, and Faith Series, which includes *Callum's Compass* (2017), *Camp Hope* (2018), and *Rarity Mountain* (March 2019). She also has a story, "Leap of Faith," in *Chicken Soup for the Soul: Step Outside Your Comfort Zone* and a novella, *Of Walls* (November 2018). Sara finds inspiration in her faith, her family, and the beauty of nature. When she isn't writing, you can find her reading, camping, and spending time outdoors with her family. To learn more about her and her work or to become a part of her email friend's group, please visit www.saralfoust.com.

CPSIA information can be obtained
at www.ICGtesting.com
Printed in the USA
LVHW031721210220
647794LV00003B/544

9 781732 904712